Shane Simmons

RAW

and
Other Stories

Twenty Tales
of Dark Crime,
Everyday Horror, and
Pitch-Black Comedy

ISBN: 978-1-988954-01-1

Published by Eyestrain Productions
eyestrainproductions.com

EYESTRAIN
PRODUCTIONS

Table of Contents

Wrangler

I KNOW, I KNOW.

I bitch and complain. I piss and moan. But I realize I've got it good. And it's not that I'm unappreciative. Circumstances have left me in an advantageous position which I use—some might say abuse—to its full extent. I have the run of the house. Or, let's be honest, mansion. Twenty-seven rooms, eight fireplaces, an indoor heated swimming pool, a hot tub, Jacuzzi, and sauna. All of it sitting on a dozen acres of lake-front property with its own boat house, tennis court and four-car garage. Oh, and of course, a heated outdoor swimming pool to dwarf its indoor cousin.

I don't have to pay a dime for any of it. My meals are included, as are most of my other basic expenses. Whatever isn't automatically covered is easily purchased with a generous allowance which arrives promptly on the first of every month.

Each morning I wake up in the master bedroom, make the long journey to the edge of my gigantic bed, across the sea of silk, and step out through the French doors to a balcony that overlooks the fairy-tale grounds. I breathe in the crisp lake air and smell the rose garden, the freshly trimmed lawn, the lilac blossoms of spring, and I rejoice in the thought: It's mine, all mine.

Except it isn't. Close, but not quite. I'm the only person here, and before you ask, no. I'm not a squatter who broke into somebody's mansion while they were away on a six-month jaunt in Europe. I have every right to be here. More than that, I have a responsibility to be here. And I take this responsibility very seriously because if I fail, it all goes away.

Mister Jasper is the real owner of the house, everything in it, and the fortune in the bank that pays for its upkeep. He is the sole inheritor and master, but I'm his caretaker. He's very independent, this Mister Jasper, and he'd live here alone if he could. But he needs me to do a lot of things for him. Light cleaning mostly, and preparing meals. Left to his own devices, he could probably go out and get his own food, but he needs me to fix him something regular, healthy and nutritious. He's hopeless with a can opener. Other than that, I manage his collection of knickknacks he likes to admire and fondle. I make sure they're readily available and don't get lost under furniture. And, of course, I supply him with cuddles on demand. I'm not really into it, but I don't think he can tell. Or if he can, he doesn't care. As long as I'm there to rub his belly, nuzzle his neck, or spoon with him, he's happy. And Mister Jasper's happiness is paramount.

You ever read one of those stories in the papers, or hear it on the news? The media loves this crap, so they report it every time it happens. Eccentric millionaire kicks the bucket and wills her entire estate to her cat. Or cats. Or sometimes a dog. "All that for a stupid house pet that would just as soon eat a dead squirrel and sleep in a pile of rags?" is the usual sort of dismayed reaction you can expect from the public before they turn the page or change the channel in disgust. There's never any sort of follow-up, but I've looked into it. And I can tell you that most of those wills get overturned by a judge. Sons, daughters, stepkids all challenge it in court. And if they don't, second cousins twice removed come out of the woodwork to dispute it. Before long, the spoils of the estate are divvied up between the surviving humans, and Fluffy or Fido, once looking at a life of luxury, gets fobbed off on the first aunt or uncle willing to take the critter in. Failing that, the dethroned successor gets chauffeured to the nearest animal shelter for a last meal of generic kibble and a lethal injection.

"It's not what she would have wanted," is something one of the family might lament out loud for anyone who cares to hear this token objection. And then they take their sparkling new inheritance and buy a car with it and forget all about the family pet that had once been named lord of the manor and heir apparent.

But sometimes, just sometimes, there's nobody to contest the will.

I expect it caught the law firm in charge of Mrs. Alicia Wimple's considerable estate by surprise when absolutely no one stepped forward to object to her very simple last will and testament that left everything in her possession—from the home and its furnishings, to the bank account and stock options—for the maintenance and happiness of her beloved tuxedo cat, Mister Jasper. An intern had been sent by the house a couple of times a day to set out some food and scoop the litter box, but eventually it became clear, if the will was not overturned, the terms set out in it must be obeyed. It was only then, six weeks after Alicia Wimple had been buried in a ceremony that saw few friends but plenty of people on her payroll in attendance, that her lawyers began an earnest search for someone who could act as a full-time caretaker to a single aging cat.

The help-wanted posting found me at my old job toiling as a worker bee for an advertising agency. A friend spotted it online and emailed me a link, largely as a joke. I only applied as a lark. The pay rate was low and the duties sounded tiresome. I arranged an interview anyway, just to see what it was all about. It seems few people applied, probably because there was never any mention of all the considerable perks that went along with the position. I only found out about them myself once the offer was on the table. They made it very easy to say yes.

What set me ahead of the other sparse candidates was my background as a wrangler. The gentlemen hired to screen applicants looked genuinely impressed when I mentioned I had worked with cats extensively. Two years earlier, the agency that employed me had been contracted for a series of television commercials for cat food—wet canned food with new-improved artificial tuna flavour as I recall. With half the crew allergic and the other half certified dog-lovers, it had fallen on me to deal with the handful of feline thespians we had recruited from death row at an animal-control facility. I got to feed and care for them over the course of the shoot, made sure they responded to their cues, and patiently ran them through their paces as they ruined take after take after take. Cats are terrible performers. They won't follow instructions, won't learn tricks, and pretty much refuse to do anything you want them to do when you want them to do it. All I could accomplish for the cat-food campaign was set the stars down on their mark and hope they did something that vaguely resembled the script so the cameras could capture it.

The job was a misery for the film crew, but I was unfazed by the experience. I got my hourly wage whether the cats behaved according to plan or not. Eventually the crew got enough usable footage to call it a wrap and the cats were sent back to the shelter— back to a cage to wait for fate to choose adoption or euthanization for them, but well groomed and well fed for their trouble.

The next campaign was for pantyhose and I quickly forgot all about my brief stint as a cat wrangler. Until it came up in the interview. Little did I know, it was my ace in the hole. The job as Mister Jasper's personal servant was on the table if I wanted it. And I wanted it the first moment I laid eyes on a picture of the house I would be living in as I performed my duties.

So began a long and luxurious string of days that ran into years. It was a happy time for me and, dare I say, a happy time for the cat as well. I didn't shirk my duties. The cat got all the attention and playtime and strokes he craved, and whenever I was satisfied that the boss was satisfied, I got to kick back and enjoy life as never before. I wasn't rich, but I had access to all the toys money could buy, and that was as-good-as in my book. The bed alone was ample compensation for my undemanding routine—deep and cozy, with linen like a heavenly cocoon. I never slept so well or so deeply. The cat concurred, and would ignore his dozen high-end cat beds in favour of sleeping at my feet each night. I would find him there most mornings, still asleep but ready to boisterously ask for his first meal of the day once I stirred.

One such morning, I found Jasper—*Mister Jasper* to those on less familiar terms—curled up on the end of the bed, his head tucked into his tail. I gave him a reassuring pat to let him know I was awake, on call, and at his service. He didn't look up, didn't purr, and wasn't breathing. His soft coat of fur was cool to my touch and the body beneath it felt stiff as a plank.

Mister Jasper, I realized, was now the late Mister Jasper.

● ● ●

What happens when you lose your meal ticket? Simple really. You get another.

Cats are a dime a dozen. There's an inexhaustible supply of them in pet stores and animal shelters. Or you can find them just running around loose in the street. And no matter how many of them get adopted, spayed or neutered, there remain whole colonies of feral cats out there making more and more kittens.

Finding another cat to replace Jasper and become the new master of the house wasn't the issue. Finding a precise match for his predecessor, however, was a very big issue. The body-double cat had to be able to withstand the scrutiny of lawyers and estate managers who swung by as a matter of routine to check on things and assure that the richest feline in the land was receiving his full due from his inheritance.

The first step was to dispose of the body. It was the one piece of evidence that would sink me and my future in the house if it was discovered. Within the hour, he was buried deep, the spade was rinsed and hanging back in the garage, and I was showered and dressed after my excavation in the dirt.

If I sound cold-hearted about ditching the remains of my constant companion in an unmarked garden grave, perhaps I should explain that Mister Jasper—*this* Mister Jasper—wasn't so constant in the companionship department. I'd been on the job for years, he had only been at it for the last seven months. This was, in fact, only the latest in a string of cats, collectively known as Mister Jasper. The original had died of old age within the first year of my tenure. It happened quite peacefully and unexpectedly. Missing for a whole day, I'd found him dead behind a sofa after tearing the place apart looking for him. There was no point in taking him to the vet, no use in seeking medical attention, and, I ultimately decided, no good to come of telling anyone what had happened.

The original Mister Jasper was buried respectfully and with all due honours in the backyard, away from prying eyes, and was replaced over a hurried weekend of auditions with a virtually identical cat recruited from an online listing, after I'd scanned through a thousand other adult cats being offered in a dozen nearby towns and cities. It was a two-hundred-mile round trip to get the newly christened Mister Jasper 2.0 settled in, but once he had the run of the place and got used to having me as a roommate, he took to his new life quite nicely. There were personality differences, of course. All cats have their own unique quirks. But there was nothing so singular about him that a casual observer, come to check on things at the house and make sure I was fulfilling my end of the bargain, would ever notice in a twenty-minute weekly inspection.

The second Jasper lasted two years, but remained feral at heart. The original had been an indoor cat, the second longed to return to the outdoors. He slipped outside several times, but the property was vast, and I had always managed to recapture him and return him to his lavish prison. We didn't fare so well the last time he escaped. A brief but vicious encounter with a coyote left Jasper the Second badly mangled and struggling for survival. I nursed him through the night, binding and tending his wounds, but he was gone by morning and buried by noon. The process of replacement began anew.

By the time the latest cat had had his fill of life, this routine was old hat to me. There was no more panic, no more rush, no more fear of discovery. Visits and inspections were strictly scheduled, and my sources for new cats were reliable and many. I knew I had nearly two whole days before the next visit of Jack Hainsworth, the lead lawyer for the estate. He made it his business to swing by once every month, above and beyond the usual house calls made by his subordinates, to personally make sure all was well with the property and its star occupant. He rarely stayed more than five minutes, which suited me. I had the distinct impression he saw more in those five minutes than anyone in his employ was capable of observing in multiples of that time. He knew, for instance, if I had moved any expensive curios, shifted any furniture, or left any doors or drawers ajar that were supposed to be shut. As yet, however, he'd been oblivious to the casting changes of the house cat over the years. As far as he knew, Mister Jasper was a good twenty years old and still going strong. It was a very advanced age for a cat, but not implausible—especially for a wealthy feline with bottomless resources to keep him happy and healthy. I figured I had as much as five more years before believability was stretched to the breaking point, and I was determined to ride out my good fortune for every day of it.

Admittedly, getting an exact match for Mister Jasper was never going to be possible. The key thing was to find a tuxedo cat of the same size with a reasonably comparable arrangement of black and white spots. Even without pinpoint accuracy, people who didn't live with the cat day in and day out wouldn't notice, provided the black to white ratio was close enough and in the same general configuration. So far, the eagle eyes of Jack Hainsworth had failed to detect the switches when they happened. As long as the cat met expectations, he was more concerned with the condition of the other estate assets that might one day go to auction, somewhere down the road.

With under forty hours to make the switch, I expected things might get tight, but I'd accomplish the feat before in less time than that. Day one was consumed with online research and phone calls. I made the rounds of the shelters and pet stores, animal rescue organizations and want ads looking for new homes for adult cats. By the time I needed to sleep for fear of passing out at the computer, I hadn't come across a single lead. There were dozens of tabbies, solid black cats, white cats, and calicos too. A few tortoise-shell cats were available, plus a broad selection of Persians and Siamese. I even found a couple of rare hypo-allergenic breeds that were usually snatched up immediately by waiting lists. But no tuxedos. Not one.

Well, okay, there was one, but he was immediately disqualified. Aside from looking mangy, with chewed-up ears and distinctly crossed eyes, he was morbidly obese and I had no time to spruce him up and put him on a diet.

I made a number of follow-up calls the next morning, pursuing a few thin hopes from the previous day. They were all quashed in short order. There was simply nothing out there for me. There weren't even any suitable neighbourhood cats to borrow temporarily.

I briefly considered opting for one of the solid-white or solid-black cats and trying to dye or bleach my way to a reasonable facsimile of Mister Jasper, but I had to dismiss that as fantasy. There was no way Hainsworth would fail to spot my improvised attempt to provide him with a paint-by-numbers version of his best client.

I resolved, in the end, for desperate measures.

Isadore—or Izzy as she was referred to by those out of earshot—lived on the edge of town, in a big house that wasn't big enough for her menagerie. She was known as the local crazy cat lady, which I always thought was unfair. Izzy is crazy in so many other ways as well. Early on in my Jasper-doppelgänger escapades, I had resorted to her services once and swore I'd never go back.

I might have called ahead to see what she had in stock, but that wasn't an option. If she had a phone, I didn't have the number. And even if I had a number and there was a phone to call, there was no guarantee Isadore would even be able to find it. Izzy was a collector, who had been collecting all her life, and she had lived to be very old. The cats were only one symptom of her pathological hoarding.

I rang the bell after my long drive to the wrong side of the tracks. The house was filthy, run-down, and stank of every liquid or solid that can come out of a cat. I hoped the doorbell and a matching cat were the only things I would have to touch.

"It's you!" Izzy declared through the screen door five minutes and five more rings later, once she had finally made her way through the canyons of unlabelled boxes and towers of stacked newspapers.

"It's me," I agreed.

"I haven't seen you around for ages now," said Izzy. Of course, she wouldn't have. Not unless I came by for a visit on purpose. She had her groceries delivered and never left the house except to score another stray or ten.

"How's your sweet kitty?" she immediately wanted to know. "The tabby."

"Tuxedo," I reminded her.

"Of course!" she said like she remembered, though I strongly doubted she could possibly have a mental index of all the cats that passed through her home.

"Dead," I said.

Izzy looked crestfallen, personally wounded by the news, even though the cat she gave me was several Jaspers ago and wasn't young when I recruited him.

"Old age," I assured her. "It was peaceful."

I didn't let on that he'd already been years in a garden grave.

"And you've come to me for a new little friend," Izzy deduced solemnly.

I nodded, and gave her the sad eyes of the grief-stricken.

"I can't say I have quite so many on hand as I usually do," she said.

There were at least a dozen cats perched in the various windows at the front of the house, all of them staring at me, like prisoners in a holding cell, wondering if they'd made bail at last. Untold dozen more were probably inside, curled up and nesting in a jungle of junk, or hiding until they heard Izzy pour more food into a wall-to-wall collection of bowls that covered most of her kitchen floor.

"I have three nice orange kitties you could choose from," she said, picturing the inventory of pets she hadn't become emotionally attached to yet.

"I was hoping for another tuxedo, just like the last one."

"I see," she nodded. "It's easier sometimes if you replace your baby with one who looks almost the same."

"I might even name him Jasper, as well," I agreed.

"There hasn't been much in the way of tuxedos of late," Izzy told me. "Can't say I have a single one in the house. There's one black cat with a single white spot on his belly. I don't suppose he'd do?"

"I really had my heart set on a match," I said, even as that heart sank. I was grasping at straws now. "I don't suppose you've seen any like it around? Strays or such? Maybe one of your neighbours has a cat like that."

I wasn't above catnapping at this point. I'd have been willing to steal someone's pet out of their yard if it came to that—or at least borrow one without permission. Only long enough to survive the next inspection and come up with a permanent replacement. Then I'd return him to where I found him. Probably.

"There's a cat colony," Izzy said after much reflection. "Out at The Old Mill."

The Mill used to be the sole factory and main employer in town, back when the local economy was fuelled by honest industry rather than the tourist dollars of rich urbanites who summered here for the lake and wintered here for the skiing. It became The "Old" Mill when it laid off everybody and shuttered its doors thirty years ago. That event nearly destroyed the town, and it was years before new money with an eye for the surrounding natural beauty began to prop the place back up with a demand for property, restaurants and inns. Izzy was one of the few who had been around long before the transition, remembered how things once were, and was never tempted to pack up and move away—mostly because packing up would have been impossible. When The Mill shut down, her life had already become buried under a mountain of mementoes, keepsakes and genuine trash she refused to part with. It was amazing to me that she ever agreed to part with the occasional cat, but then I guess she didn't consider them possessions so much as transient lodgers.

"I was out there last week, checking for strays," she continued. "Most of them are pretty wild. They wouldn't come near me."

I didn't blame them. Life on the prowl, subsisting on a diet of mice and birds, masterless and free, sounded better than being caged by a crazy cat lady. I hoped they might sense I could offer them a better life. The best life any cat could hope to have, in fact.

"As I recall," said Izzy, "one of them was a tuxedo. I couldn't get a good look, but he might be what you're looking for if he'll let you get close."

● ● ●

The path up to The Mill was muddy and overgrown. Much of the area had been paved when it was in operation, but in the years since, the concrete base had become cracked and split open, allowing for weeds, brush and even a few small trees to grow up through the gaps. The brick building was vast, filling several acres of land, with no other industries nearby to compete with its dominant-landmark status. Not a single window was left unbroken and most of the doors were missing, offering easy access to the skeletal remains.

I stepped through the debris inside, careful not to slip and fall on loose rubble or tread on one of the rusty nails that had been shed by the old wooden beams. The equipment and machines were long gone, but the place remained filled with potential tetanus or injury.

I spent ten minutes wandering around before I spotted my first cat, eyeing me suspiciously from around a corner. Slowing my pace, I checked any quick moves that might scare off skittish felines. As I drew closer to the heart of The Mill, and my eyes adjusted to the dim light, I began to spot additional cats every few paces. They all seemed wary of my presence, but none was alarmed enough to run or give up their choice spot within the derelict ruin.

Three more passages got me to the core of the building. Hundreds used to work there at a time, in shifts that ran day and night. Now there was nothing left but peeling lead paint and walls that were probably brimming with asbestos. I wondered how many toxins I might be exposing myself to, and how many more might be released if the crumbling edifice suffered a partial collapse. My eyes shifted to the corners of the ceiling, wondering how sound the structure still was, and worrying about the mould spores and carcinogenic particles that might be raining down on me while I was breathing the tainted air.

That's when I saw him, perched on top of a stone wall that used to support rafters and roof but was now left exposed and freestanding. The tuxedo was perfect—or at least as perfect as I was ever going to find as the final hours of my deadline ticked away. He had the obligatory white paws, the white-tipped tail, and the general correct facial pattern that would allow him to pass for Jasper. Being a wild cat, he was a bit rough around the edges. I could tell, even from a dozen paces away, that he didn't have the silky fur of a pampered indoor cat, but I could work with that. Grooming would go a long way towards improving his appearance. Maybe, in time, I could get him to trust me enough to attempt a bath. At any rate, a good comb-out to get rid of the loose fur and untangle any mats would beautify him enough to get through a cursory inspection.

Right then, my only task was to draw him in close enough to stuff him into a caged cat carrier and bring him home. I'd stopped at a supermarket on the way for the best bait I could think of. My pockets were filled with a collection of single-serving cans of salmon. I opened the first one with the pull tab and poured the fish juice across the floor before setting the can down as an offering. The salmon-infused water was pungent and the scent spread quickly, attracting attention. There were soon many more feline eyes peering at me from around corners and under spaces between the floorboards. They must have all been hungry, all tempted by the promise of a good meal, all calculating whether they should risk approaching the intruding human in order to get at the tantalizing fish meat.

Chasing off the others while trying to draw just one wouldn't work, so I started opening more cans and flaking their contents out with my finger until I was completely surrounded by chunks of pink salmon and a powerful fishy stink. It was several minutes before the first and bravest of the cats crept forward and dared to gnaw at the piece of food that had fallen the farthest from me. When I remained still and didn't make a sound in response, the others started to find their courage and, one after the next, came out of hiding and stepped forward to receive their bounty.

The tuxedo remained on his perch, watching over the scene, contemplating, calculating. I could tell he wanted the food, but he wasn't so keen to give up his safe spot as overseer. Piece by piece, I watched the salmon disappear down the greedy maws of at least twenty cats, and I was concerned there would soon be none left for the one cat of the bunch I wanted to dine. I'm sure he was equally concerned by the diminishing buffet. Finally, before it was all gone, he decided to chance it and leapt down from his perch. He boldly strode over, fixated on one particularly large and tempting flake only a few feet in front of me. Seeing I had molested none of the other cats so far, he assumed he was safely invisible in the herd and helped himself eagerly, taking big bites and throwing them back with a hen-pecking jerk of his head.

"Good boy," I assured him, and reached out slowly with one hand.

I stroked his back with the tips of my fingers and he didn't resist. Even after he had downed the final crumbs of his share of the fish, he stuck around, enjoying the first attention any human had lavished on him in years, if ever. With little encouragement, he pressed his head against my hand and leaned into it when I rubbed one ear. Shifting my feet, I edged closer and eased my other hands under his front legs so I could lift him into my lap. I was prepared to grab hold tightly if I had to, but there was no attempt to escape. As starved as he was for a good meal, my tuxedo was equally starved for affection.

As I scratched under his chin and worked his other ear with my thumb. I scanned the cat's coat for any hint of parasites, injuries, or other obvious signs of neglect that would get me fired if they were noticed and blamed on me. Other than a few knots of hair, the candidate seemed to be in good working order. Things were looking up.

Rising to my feet, cradling the cat in my arms, I started to make my way back outside where I had left the cat carrier. I hadn't brought it in for fear of freaking out the whole cat colony. There was a good chance some of them, once owned and cared for, would remember that such dreaded devices were employed for traumatic trips to the vet. The sight of one could have caused snowballing panic, and I wouldn't have seen another whisker. For a moment, I dared to hope I would make it all the way back to my car without incident. The tuxedo seemed content to make the journey. He was even purring.

Then I heard the alien voice, echoing off the bricks of the connecting, cavernous rooms.

"You a cop?"

I couldn't tell where it was coming from, other than it was in the building with me. I started towards the nearest door and found it blocked by a man stepping into my path. He was dishevelled, rough around the edges, but not dirty. His clothes weren't torn, probably hadn't been slept in—much—and his sneakers were new, clean, and of a fashionable, trendy style that cost too much money for mere running shoes. I might have expected to run into a homeless person or two, but the young fellow before me wasn't camping out in the desolation.

"You after my stash?" he asked, piercing me with an accusatory stare.

Any hope that he was a harmless urban explorer, fascinated by decaying, crumbling monuments of bygone eras, faded. He was here on business, and I was trespassing. Looking at a vacant spot in the corner, he didn't wait for a response.

"Where's my stash?" he demanded.

In my quest for the right cat, I had inadvertently stumbled upon the wrong place at the wrong time. It seemed that this was a drop spot for a local drug dealer. There was probably a sale pending and he was returning to raid his wares—likely a box or backpack with carefully divided bags of whichever poison he was peddling. Instead, he'd found me, unexpected and unwanted, invading the space he'd claimed for the day or the week. Either he was misremembering where he'd left his goods, or someone else had helped themselves to the store before I ever got there. Whatever the case, he was holding me responsible.

"I didn't touch your stash!" I claimed, probably too shrilly. I worried the knee-jerk denial made me sound guilty of the falsely accused crime.

"What the hell are you doing in our place, man?"

Our place. I didn't like the suggestion of multiple dealers. Dealers who were probably also users, strung out and paranoid on who-knows-what. It meant more comings and goings, more on the way to ambush me, corner me, kill me for what I hadn't even done.

"I'm adopting a cat!" I explained, hoping the cat in my arms would lend credibility to my claim. It didn't.

"I know no damn cat took it!" he shouted. "Where's it at?"

How much was this guy's stash worth, I wondered? A few hundred dollars? A few thousand? I didn't suppose it would do much good to try to convince him that I wasn't interested in his stash because I was about to lose my own, worth millions.

The angry dealer reached behind his back and pulled a long knife out from under the waistband of his track pants.

"You show me where you put it or I'm gonna gut you lookin' for it," he said.

I realized then that I was about to lose a lot more than my job, my mansion, my pools—indoors and out. I was about to lose my life, which is just the same as losing everything all in one shot. He wouldn't need to stick me with that knife more than once to get the job done. The Mill was much too isolated for anyone to hear me cry for help. Even if his cut left me mobile, it would be a long crawl back to the car. If I didn't bleed to death on the way, I was sure the inevitable infection from the filthy blade would finish me off.

My fight-or-flight instinct was kicking in hard, and I liked the flight option much better. The only problem with that course of action was that the criminal and his knife were blocking the sole passage out. When he took a step forward, blade extended while he judged where to make his incision, the choice was made for me. I didn't know the first thing about fighting or self-defence—hadn't been in so much as a shoving match since the playground. Nevertheless, I seized the moment to lash out with the only weapon I had on hand—the stray cat in my arms. With no warning, to either the drug dealer or the cat, I launched the animal right at him with force.

The tuxedo flew through the air. There was a split moment of black and white limbs, whipping about wildly, before the cat reflexes engaged and prepared for the best available landing. Hitting the dealer mid-body, the cat latched on with his fish-hook claws, clinging for anything to prevent a fall, digging through thin layers of clothing and finding flesh underneath. The thug screamed and the cat howled in response. Rather than repel off him and flee back the way he came, the cat decided to head in the opposite direction, climbing over the top of the man, one pawful of flesh at a time, trying to get to his back by way of his face. Claws scratched their way to firm footholds that cut much deeper and even more painfully, until he'd traversed right over the punk's scalp and halfway down his back. Only then did he disengage and push off from the base of the man's spine, sprinting for cover.

In only a few seconds, the drug dealer had been sliced and diced dozens of times over by pinprick claws much sharper than the weapon he had threatened me with. He stood, frozen in place by the pain, wincing for a few vital seconds while I watched the first expanding stains of blood appear on his clothes where the cuts soaked into the fibres. If I was going to escape, it was now or never. The wrath he would direct at me once he recovered from the initial shock of the tag-team assault would be fierce.

He was still blocking the door, so I barrelled straight into him, knocking him to the floor and stepping right on him in my haste to clear some distance between us. There were angry, incomprehensible shouts in my wake, but I never looked back to see if the enraged hoodlum was back on his feet and giving chase. I was outside again in a matter of seconds, bounding across the pavement and leaping into the brush beyond, losing myself in decades of weeds and the most recent crop of determined saplings.

I put a quarter of a mile between myself and The Mill before stopping to catch my breath. Crouching down in the tall grass, out of sight, I listened closely for anyone approaching. My car, I guessed, was parked along the road another fifty yards to my right. If someone came after me, it would be another sprint. Even if I won the race, I'd still have to unlock the door, get inside, and start the engine before represent-atives of the small-time local drug cartel caught up with me. It would be very close.

I could hear birdsong in the distant trees, and the whisper of a slight breeze playing with the tips of the grass. There was no more shouting, no more curses, no more baseless accusations or oaths of retribution. I was certain I was being hunted, silently, somewhere in that overgrown field.

At last I heard a noise that confirmed my suspi-cions—the distinct sound of dry grass being pressed down underfoot. The sound grew closer and I held my breath, hoping all the towering weeds would offer me enough cover for any onlookers to pass me by without notice.

In my growing terror, I became certain the hunter was zeroing in on my exact location. The noise was so near, yet when I looked up at the skyline over the grassy forest, I could see no human heads bobbing across the horizon as they beat the bushes for me. I was almost ready to bolt when I felt a sudden rough pain in my fingertips, like the vowed revenge against me had already begun in the form of a teeny-tiny belt sander.

I saw, as I had feared, that I'd been discovered.

It was the tuxedo cat who had tracked me down, drawn by the lingering scent of the fish juice that soiled my hands. He was licking my fingers greedily, trying to extract the final hints of flavour.

"Sweetie," I smiled, relieved, "I have all you can eat back home."

● ● ●

The cat carrier, as I expected, was not particularly popular. The car ride, even less so. But once we were back home, with more food and fresh water in the offing, the tuxedo decided that perhaps he wasn't in such dire straits after all.

There was some resistance to the idea of being groomed by a human, but once I got the comb through his coat a few times, the cat decided he liked it and arched his back into it. I expected a full-blown bath in the relatively near future wouldn't go down as well, but that was a worry for a later date. Right now, the top priority was to achieve "presentable" by the most slap-dash means possible. A visit from Jack Hainsworth was only a couple of hours away.

It was a miracle the cat wasn't swimming with fleas. I could tell with one look that the newest Jasper's ear canals were filled with mites—common among cats born wild. Daily treatment with some ointment from the vet would clear that up within a couple of weeks. I didn't expect a close enough examination to spot them. Not unless something else tipped off the lawyer that the business-as-usual scene was contrived.

Hainsworth arrived at the end of the day, as the sun was setting, shortly after his office had closed for the day. We exchanged our usual pleasantries, as paid business associates who aren't friendly otherwise do, and he made the rounds of the house, making certain everything was in good order. For all my efforts over the last frantic days, he didn't even look for the cat, didn't so much as ask after him. He was almost out the door without making a single inquiry about Mister Jasper's well-being, which suited me fine. But then, in those few seconds before he would have been safely outside and gone for another month, the newest king of the castle strolled by. I held my breath, hoping that my quick-fix makeover would save the day.

"I see you've adopted a new companion," commented Hainsworth.

I realized then that he didn't even recognize the cat I had procured as the real Jasper—had, in fact, assumed I had taken it upon myself to find Jasper another feline to pal around with. I considered agreeing with him, but then if he asked to see the true master of the house, I was sunk. This, for better or worse, *had* to be the one. I tried to sell Hainsworth on the lie as casually as I could.

"No, that's just Jasper. Same old, same old."

I opened the front door and held it for Hainsworth, but he didn't turn to leave. Instead, he took more time than he ever had before to scrutinize the cat with his immaculate powers of observation.

"Perhaps if I squint, but no," he said at last. "Not a terribly good likeness, this one. I take it the last cat is no longer with us?"

"Of course he's with us," I protested feebly, "he's right there."

Hainsworth ignored my attempts to recover a lost cause.

"Old age, natural causes, I hope."

"What are you talking about?" I tried to laugh. "There's only one cat here. The same cat that's always been here. A little older, a little worse for wear maybe, but alive and well as you can see."

"Stop," said Hainsworth as I babbled.

"I guess he could use a bath..." I tried.

"Just stop," he said again. And I did.

"You know?"

"Of course I know. Everyone knows," said Hainsworth. "The trust manager, the accountants, my entire firm. Not to mention handymen, maintenance men, groundskeepers—all the people who collect a fee for keeping this estate running and pristine, ostensibly for the benefit and enjoyment of a single cat. Everyone down to the pool boy and the chimney sweeps who stop by twice a year know."

I tried to think if there was anyone who hadn't made the list, wasn't in on my deepest, darkest deceit.

"The gardener?" I suggested after much thought.

"You bury seven cats in the garden and expect the gardener not to notice? Of course the gardener knows. He was the first to know and passed the information on to me."

I was busted. Thoroughly busted, exposed, laid bare. Mentally, I was already packing my bags. It wouldn't take long. I didn't actually own anything.

"So why am I still here?" I asked.

"For the same reason we're all here," Hainsworth patiently explained. "It pays. That cat, and all the salaries and fees and invoices surrounding it, is supporting at least six families, putting ten students through college, and keeping three entire businesses and one moderately sized local bank in the black. That cat can never die. It would be an economic catastrophe. If word got out that Mister Whiskers..."

"Jasper," I felt obliged to correct.

"Whatever the hell its stupid name is... If word ever got out that he'd passed on, I wouldn't be the least bit surprised to see the Dow Jones Industrial Average take an instant triple-digit dip. That's how much money and prosperity is tied up in that cat's inheritance."

"So I'm not fired," I eventually dared to confirm.

"Of course not. You're doing a better job than any of us could have hoped. Keep it up."

Hainsworth stepped outside and pressed his keychain to remotely unlock his expensive car—paid for by the good graces of Mister Jasper's continued existence, no doubt.

"I know it can't be easy duplicating your charge," he told me, "but try to make this one last. It must be exhausting trying to find replacements all the time."

"How'd you spot that this wasn't the same cat as the last Mister Jasper?" I called after him as he got behind the wheel. "I thought I got a perfect match this time."

"Nipples," he said quite simply.

"Huh?" was my best response.

"They're rather prominent, don't you think? I believe *Mister* Jasper is pregnant."

Jack Hainsworth started his car and drove away down the oval drive. By the time I saw him again, I was likely to have an entire litter of kittens to attend to—all of them heirs to the heir. I thought about how I might soon be waking up in my gigantic luxury bed with half a dozen cats pinning me under the covers—how the demands for food and playtime and belly rubs would double and triple and multiply even more.

Oh well, I concluded, the estate was large, with room enough for us all.

Heads Will Roll

THE SNAKE LAY in the middle of the double-lane highway. Head, body, flattened middle, more body and rattle. A two-foot length had been squashed paper thin by the sparse traffic since it first became roadkill while trying to cross the pavement on the blistering hot day. So far the wheels had all missed the best part. Ruby didn't even bother with the spade for this one. She let one more car roll over the snake and then stepped out into the road. She could see straight down the highway for miles, and the next vehicle was still a couple of minutes away.

She grabbed the snake by the tail and peeled it off the asphalt with a single sharp flick of her wrist. Once she was safely back on the shoulder, she twisted the head around three times and tore it free. The head went in the sack. She threw the rest of the body into the dry brown brush just off the side of the road.

The sack was getting heavy. She'd have to unload early. That made it a good day.

Kelly's Diner was another couple of miles off. She knew there was a piece of pie waiting for her there. There always was. If she was lucky, and the road continued to be fruitful, she'd have pie in her belly and another head or two in her sack before the hour was up.

● ● ●

"Oh shit," said May at the sight of Earl walking through the door. It was a sentiment often repeated.

May had worked tables at the diner for so long, she had been acquainted with Kelly—the namesake of the truck stop—and he'd been dead many years now. She made a point of knowing all the regulars, or the irregulars as she thought of them. Most of the men in the rigs would drop by once or twice a month at best, roughly around the mid-point of their coast-to-coast hauls. She'd recognize faces, learn names, and earn a better tip with the personal touch. Hardly any locals came there to eat. Few people called that lonely stretch of road home, and the nearest town, ten miles away, offered nicer restaurants if you were inclined to dine out.

Earl, it seemed, had decided to become a local. He had a van with a bedroll in the back, and May had spotted it parked here and there between her shifts. He never strayed very far from the diner. It was where he ate most days and where he did all his business. May had seen his type before and knew what he was after when she saw him chatting up truckers, interrupting their meals with unsolicited small talk, and sometimes having an arranged meeting out in the lot between the rigs. Only two types of drifters did that—hustlers and dealers. May hadn't been sure which one Earl was until she saw him pass a small plastic bag to one of the drivers under the cover of a handshake.

Nearly half the take at the diner was from coffee sales. Truckers lived on joe, but it wasn't enough to keep all of them going through the hours and miles they were expected to keep. The pill poppers were an easy market for anyone slinging speed. Earl looked to have a whole case of it stashed in his van. May didn't resent any hustler or dealer their living, but Earl was another matter. He was just plain unpleasant, and she couldn't wait for him to run out of pills so he would fuck off down the road to restock and set up elsewhere.

"Coffee, eggs, bacon," said Earl as he sat down at the counter. May suspected he always chose a stool rather than a table just to give her a front-row look at his sickening eating habits.

"Morning, Earl," she replied for the sake of conversation as she grabbed the pot of old coffee that had been sitting on the heating pad for too many hours.

"It ain't morning if it's past noon and it's damn near one," said Earl.

"Good afternoon, then," May corrected herself, pouring him a cup she hoped would taste thick and bitter.

Earl looked around for any prospective customers. Business at the diner was slow so that meant business for Earl was bound to be slower.

"Not many folks in the old shithole today, is there? You run out of grease back there?"

"I'll tell Wayne to cut an extra slice just for you," said May, pushing through the door to the kitchen.

Wayne was on the grill, flipping burgers for a phoned-in takeout.

"Scrambled eggs," said May. "And bacon."

"Who's come in?" asked Wayne.

"It's Earl. Again."

"Burn the bacon?"

"And spit in the eggs," said May before returning to her post.

● ● ●

Ruby looked down at the armadillo on the shoulder. It had been struck on the road, but had managed to hobble off to one side, saving itself from another hit.

"This'n ain't quite dead," she noted aloud. "But there's no rules sayin' they can't be fresh."

The armadillo was still trying to get to the bushes, but it would never make it. Fool thing would have been better to lie down in the lane and let some eighteen wheeler finish the job. Better for him, less suffering, but Ruby would have been robbed of a perfectly good head most likely.

She put the blade of the flat-bottom spade against the roadkill's throat and brought her foot down hard on the right-hand tread, clipping its head off and ending it. She scraped it away from the body, just to be sure she'd cut all the way through and it wasn't still attached by any skin or gristle. Once it was clear, she plucked it off the bed of gravel by the ear and threw it into the sack with the rest.

The medical research lab up at the university campus paid five dollars a head if it was in good enough shape to dissect the brain. Sometimes she'd find roadkill that had had their skulls squashed flat, either by the car that hit it, or the next one to come along. They were a waste. Others got their heads clipped by a bumper and she had to make a judgement call whether the lab would accept them or not. Unless there were brains obviously oozing out, she'd err on the side of optimism and take the head anyway. If the lab rejected any, they made her take them away with her, but there was a good tall fence to chuck the rejects over on the way back from the campus.

The day had been all varmints. Nothing that qualified as a critter. Critters were bigger and paid more—not much more, but enough to make Ruby excited when she spotted a dead deer or large dog. The distinction between varmint and critter was subjective, and the research lab had a more technical term for it that Ruby didn't understand, so she mostly went by size and how her granddaddy used to differentiate.

A cow was certainly big enough to qualify as a critter. She once delivered a whole cow head. It only paid double, even though it weighed damn near thirty pounds and required a separate trip. It was hell getting it off, but Ruby managed it in the end, though she wound up bloody head to toe. On the way back, she figured she might as well go and get bloodier before the police came by to drag the carcass away. Using the spade once more, she hacked off a few good jagged hunks of meat from the flank that made for fine barbeque that night.

Thinking of those foraged steaks made Ruby hungry, and hunger made her anticipate the waiting pie. Dessert first or second, it didn't matter. It was always the right time for free food. The diner was only a hundred yards away now. There was no more roadkill between here and there, so Ruby slung her sack over her shoulder, gripped her spade by the middle of the handle, and marched the rest of the way to the spot where the shoulder pulled back from the highway and dipped into the truck-lined parking lot of Kelly's.

● ● ●

"Jesus H. Fuckaduck, what is that stink?" declared Earl through a mouth stuffed full of bacon and eggs.

May saw it was Ruby with her sack of she-didn't-want-to-know-what slung over her shoulder. The flies were chasing her so she probably had a full load. Whatever she was scavenging, it was surely a hazard and May was always worried one of her visits would coincide with a health department inspection. Still, she didn't have the heart to kick her out. Ruby was all alone in the world and could barely care for herself. It brought out the mother in May.

"Honey, I'll get you your pie, but you're gonna have to eat it out back, okay?"

She didn't wait for a response. Ruby never had anything to say. Instead, May went straight into the kitchen to fetch yesterday's dessert. The remaining slices were still good enough to eat, even in the summer heat, just not fresh enough to serve to paying customers. Making a charity of the pie-of-the-day left-overs had been a tradition since May had first found Ruby picking through the diner's dumpster for scraps nearly three years ago.

"Hardly seems right," said Wayne, who had only been on the grill for a couple of months, "free pie or not, making the girl eat it out by the trash."

"She don't mind none. Smell out there oughta come up roses compared to that sack she carries around."

May brought out a slice of lemon meringue and found Earl talking at Ruby. She was ignoring him, but that didn't put him off.

"What's a young thing like you doing way out here in the middle of nowhere? I didn't hear nobody pull up, and don't tell me you walked in off the highway."

"Ruby," interrupted May, "come 'round back now, hon. I'll fetch you a fork."

● ● ●

Ruby sat on the curb next to the toilets at the back of the diner. Her stringy yellow hair dangling down in front of her chipped white plate, forming a privacy curtain as she shovelled heaping forkfuls of pie into her mouth. It was a private enough place to eat until Earl finished his late breakfast and came to use the facilities. He resumed their one-sided chat as soon as he spotted the girl.

"I got the key to the head," said Earl, holding up the block of wood labeled "Men's" and the key that was knotted to it. "You wanna come in there with me and have us some good times?"

Ruby didn't respond. The pie was gone, but she was still poking at the crust crumbs with the tip of a finger, bringing each one to her mouth until the plate was clean.

"I got money if that's what it takes."

That offer didn't get a response either. Ruby already had all the money she needed. A sack full of it. She just needed to swap it for a fistful of fives.

"What the hell's wrong with you? Don't you know a fair deal when you see it?"

Earl had gone as far as roughly grabbing Ruby by the arm in an effort to pull her to her feet when May popped back out of the service door.

"Leave her be," she told Earl firmly. "The girl's a bit simple, is all."

"Don't she talk none?"

"She talks just fine, 'cept she only ever talks to herself."

"She don't think the rest of us is worth talkin' to?"

"Maybe she's picky about who she cares to converse with."

It was enough to get Earl to continue about his business in the bathroom. Once the door was shut and locked behind him, May spoke to Ruby alone.

"You want another slice of pie before I feed it to the dumpster, hon?"

Ruby said nothing, but held up her empty plate for May to refill.

● ● ●

Earl hung around the diner for another hour, but didn't order anything more than free refills of coffee. A few times, May caught sight of him soliciting other customers, engaging them in light conversation, talking about the weariness of the road, and ultimately asking if they needed any sort of pick-me-up. There were no nibbles until May came out of the kitchen with a club sandwich in one hand and a BLT in the other and saw that Earl had suddenly vanished.

"Good," was all she had to say about that before hitting the floor to serve other, better customers.

• • •

"This'll perk you right up," said Earl, proud of his product. "One of these will see you through to morning."

After hours of nothing, Earl now had two buyers out in the parking lot. They didn't look like truckers or professional drivers of any sort. They were a couple of boys who probably just wanted the stamina to party all night and stay awake so they could reap the benefits of the various other narcotics they'd be popping, snorting or shooting. Earl didn't care. Whether it was for work or recreation, a sale was a sale, and everybody's money was good.

One of the kids seemed more interested in looking over Earl's shoulder than checking out the baggie of six pills being offered. Earl had left the sliding door of the van open, and the boy was nosy.

"That thing full?" he asked Earl.

The kid had his eye on the battered blue suitcase Earl had retrieved his samples from. He was usually more cautious about dipping into his stash in front of clients, but the day had been so slow, he'd been anxious to get some new money in his pocket.

"Nah," he lied. "Just the dregs. I gotta make a run out of state to my supplier."

The boys nodded knowingly.

"But you need me to hook you up, I'll still be around for a while," said Earl.

He didn't want to get knocked over, but he also didn't want to chase off potential repeat customers by overselling the claim he was light. There were nearly a hundred bags with six pills per in the case, and he wanted to unload them all before making a trip for more.

"We good?" Earl asked, looking to seal the deal.

The two boys paid up and took their goods. Earl started breathing again and resolved to be more cautious as they walked away. He hadn't been packing ever since he sold his gun for enough seed money to get started in the distribution business. If those two had decided to jump him, steal his stash, roll him for his wallet and kick the shit out of him for good measure, there wasn't much he would have been able to do to stop them.

"I guess they was truckers after all," Earl commented to himself when he saw the pair barrel out of the parking lot. It wasn't a rig, it was a pick-up. A rusty beater with oversized tires for off-roading. The one on the passenger side stuck his arm out the window and waved at him. The driver honked the horn that played the first couple of bars of an old cavalry charge and took a sharp right, roaring away down the highway.

● ● ●

"I make it sixty dollars, Ruby. That's a good haul."

One of the university post-grads, now working on a Master's degree, had unloaded the sack of roadkill heads and tallied them up. A first-year student had the unenviable task of sorting them based on a species and freshness. The heads were all promising, with no rejects, but the uniformity of size was slightly disappointing.

"Nothing bigger out there lately? We could sure use a deer or a coyote."

"Critters gone scarce," Ruby said. It sounded like a response, but she was only talking to herself. "Varmints been aplenty. Got nothin' but varmints all week."

There were other scavengers who supplied the university, mostly farm hands looking to make an extra buck when livestock died or got slaughtered, but Ruby was by far the most prolific. There was better work to be had, with better pay, even for someone of Ruby's limited capabilities. But her needs were few, and she made her own schedule with no one to answer to.

"Yeah," said the post-grad, realizing she hadn't been addressing him—had hardly even heard him speak. "Well, you keep up the good work, now."

He set out a stack of twelve fives on the counter. Ruby took them and folded them into her front pocket, never counting. She collected her sack and left without another word or look.

● ● ●

By the time Earl called it quits a few hours later, he'd only managed to move one more bag—that one to a familiar driver who had bought from him a week ago on his way to the west coast. Now that he was headed back east, he needed a refill, but only enough to see him home, not enough to make the day particularly profitable.

Earl was tired, but he didn't want to crash at the diner. He'd done that the first few nights, but then a cop had come around to run him off and he didn't want to give John Law an excuse to search his van. There was a campground farther down the highway. Most nights he'd just as soon pull over on the side of the road or up some dirt trail, but for thirty bucks he could park across from some scenery and have access to toilets, a shower and an ice machine. Once or twice a week, depending on cash flow, he'd indulge himself and call it a business expense.

He was five minutes away from the diner when he noticed he no longer had the road to himself. One moment his was the only vehicle in sight, the next there was somebody behind him coming up fast. He couldn't make out who it was. The driver-side mirror was cracked and the windows in the rear door were a haze of dust.

The other driver switched to the left-hand lane and started to overtake Earl at nearly twice his speed. He glanced out his window and all he saw was a wall of brown only inches away. No, not brown, rust. The last thing he heard, before the horrible scrape of metal grinding into his side, was a distinct bugle call, spurring men to charge.

The van was no match for the power under the pickup truck's hood. Earl swerved off the road and ran over the dip in the drainage ditch like it wasn't even there. The van took the hit well enough, but all four of the tires blew. Once it landed in the field beyond, the rims proved useless on rocks and dirt and the van tipped right over on its side and ploughed a great gouge in the baked earth.

To his surprise, Earl found himself uninjured. He'd probably pulled every muscle in his body tensing up for the crash, but he wouldn't feel that for hours. The important thing now was that nothing was broken or bleeding.

It wasn't an accident. He knew that much before the van even came to a full stop. Earl pushed up on the driver's door and let it hang off to one side as he climbed out. The rusted pickup had pulled over and he could see the two boys out and walking towards him already. Earl leapt down from the side of the van and ran for it. He didn't want to give them an excuse to finish the job.

There was nowhere to hide, so Earl kept on running and never looked back. He didn't need to because he knew exactly what he'd see. Those two kids would be helping themselves to the rest of his stash and whatever else struck their fancy in the van. Well, to hell with them. They could have it and the whole shitbox to sell for scrap too. So long as they didn't catch him and take the modest bank roll he'd saved for himself, he could hitch a ride back to his supplier and start all over again. Maybe he'd even be a few bucks ahead. The important thing was that he'd stay alive to deal another day.

Earl made it to the highway but never slowed his pace. He would run until he found a good spot to lay low, or another vehicle to flag down for a lift to town. The kids who had run him off would be back at their truck by now. He anticipated the sound of slamming doors and the engine starting. It took a few seconds longer than he thought, but these noises were immediately followed by a distant squeal of wheels. That would be them pulling a sharp one-eighty and heading back where they came from, away from the mark they'd just robbed blind and any witnesses who might come across the scene on the road up ahead. Good riddance!

Earl listened to the growl of the souped-up engine. The two in the cab would be just as souped-up on their windfall of speed that night, he figured. There was something wrong with the engine noise, however. It wasn't diminishing, it was getting louder. Too late, Earl realized they hadn't turned back. They were coming his way and were about to fly right past him. Or almost right past him. They just had to add injury to insult, the shits. A short tug on the wheel was all it took, and the front bumper punched Earl's legs out from under him at the knees, leaving him broken and bent at the side of the road. He could hear their laughter, even above the diesel roar.

● ● ●

It was getting dark by the time Earl came to. Any vehicles that might have driven by would never have seen him lying in the tall dry grass where he landed. He tried to get up and regretted it. Both his legs had been broken by the impact and there were bones sticking out of his skin. He counted himself lucky none of them had cut through an artery. Everything below his waist felt like a lead weight, but at least there was no pain.

Earl knew at once he wouldn't be going anywhere, but he would have to at least move himself a few feet to get out of the grass and close enough to the highway to be spotted. Digging his fingers into the dirt and dragging himself forward a few inches at a time was excruciating. He may have been numb through most of this body, but everything from his shoulders up was in agony. It was a relief when at last he felt gravel in his hand and was able to pull himself clear of the weeds. Someone would spot him now, for sure. Even if the sun finished going down before the next car passed, headlights would pick him up. They'd see a man lying at the side of the road and they'd stop.

A car wasn't what came upon him first. There was someone walking along the edge of the road, against the normal flow of traffic, although there was no traffic to be seen anywhere. They had the whole highway to themselves, Earl and this lone pedestrian, out in the middle of nowhere, in a place nobody ever saw except as a blur flying past their window.

"Help me," Earl said, once the person was within earshot. "I'm hurt bad."

Ruby looked down at him, at the spot he'd struggled so hard to crawl to. His spine was broken halfway up his back, folding him backwards so all his ribs were trying to pop through the buttons on his shirt. He could still move one arm, and he used it to reach for her, pleading as he touched his fingertips to the bare toes sticking out the tips of her sandals.

He gasped instructions. "Call an ambulance."

Ruby just kept staring, evaluating, saying nothing. He tried again.

"Please get help," he said again, this time begging. "I'm all twisted up."

Ruby finished assessing the situation and nodded. She'd only that moment come to a definite conclusion. Critter.

"This'n ain't quite dead," she commented. "But there's no rules sayin' they can't be fresh."

She put the blade of the flat-bottom spade against the roadkill's throat. Earl kept pawing at her toes until she raised her foot up out of his reach. The last he saw of those toes, they were coming back down, straight at him. Then there was only gravel, asphalt, darkness.

Bayonet Baby

"IT'S WAR," I announced to the room.

My co-workers were unsurprisingly cynical. They had seen too many false starts, been disappointed too many times.

"Not an insurgency?"

"No," I assured them.

"Not an uprising, or a mass protest, or a period of civil unrest?"

"No."

"The army's not just testing their arsenal or performing manoeuvres or rattling their sabres?"

"No."

"Don't tell me it's a goddamn police action," said one of them spitefully. So-called police actions were particularly unpopular in our profession.

"No, it's war. A real one. Declared and everything."

It had just come over the wire. I was the first to get it. After the usual round of disbelief, the room fell silent as it sunk in. There had been weeks of escalation and tension. New bodies littered the streets almost daily. Everyone could feel how volatile the situation was, how close it all was to exploding. Now that the inevitable had happened, it didn't seem real.

Somebody in the room said, "I have fifty bucks that says we'll hear they've started bayonetting babies before the day is out."

No one took that bet. None of us was that stupid.

● ● ●

It's a piece of propaganda that crops up early in every war. Only the pointy weapon being plunged into all those innocent babes in orphanages and hospitals and refugee camps changes, depending on the time and the place. In the era of the Roman Empire untold thousands of babies were flung into the air and caught on spears as a popular game for bored legionnaires. By the time the medieval knights laid siege to each other's castles, those hapless babies found themselves on the end of pikes. In recent guerilla actions around the world, the machete became a popular tool for baby butchery.

No matter how many strategic objectives an invading army may have to deal with on a tight schedule, they always seem to miraculously find the time to make a side trip to go bayonet some babies. Civilians across the globe are suitably horrified, because every-body can get behind the general concept that bayonetting babies is a bad thing. In this way, consent for a brand new war is won quickly and efficiently. The problem is, it never actually happens. A lot of despicable, ugly things go on in war, but no army has ever been so single-mindedly evil as to specifically target newborns for pincushion practice. Especially at the start of war, when the soldiers are still bright-eyed and bushy-tailed and eager to win lots of glory and medals. Genocidal behaviour takes a while longer to happen, cropping up only after long months of combat, once bitterness and resentment over the whole war machine sets in. Even then, if any babies get killed it's only because they've been swept up in the general carnage that begins once the initial novelty of war wears off.

So where do all the bayonetted-baby reports come from, if not actual orphanages and hospitals and refugee camps? They come from offices. Offices like ours.

● ● ●

Our building is located in a rare corner of the world where a shot has never been fired in anger. At least, not for political reasons. As a result, the design of this mid-town tower is a gleaming combination of glass and plaster. It's very pretty and very expensive. And it wouldn't last a week in a battle-torn country where mortar shells land randomly and tanks rumble down the streets on patrol. The sixth floor is dedicated to conflicts pending and in flux. We have fifty cubicles in total, each with its own agent stationed inside. Each cubicle is dedicated to its very own war, insurrection, genocide or coup. We don't have enough cubicles. Never have. The suits on the seventh floor keep promising us more dividing walls and more staff, but they never deliver. Half of us are doubled up on our caseloads at any given moment and I'm usually one of them.

Today I had an interview scheduled with the first promising refugee we were able to get out of the new warzone on a direct flight. It's important to pull our sources before a warzone goes hot. Once the real shooting begins, the logistics of extraction get complicated and it can be days before we're able to bring in a viable witness. For our purposes, she was ideal—twenty-three and photogenic, with a face that looked plausible, earnest and pained, even in her passport.

The receptionist showed her to my cubicle and she sat down opposite me in a generic office supply-store seat, equally uncomfortable as my own, but minus the wheels to roll around on. The reconfigurable walls of the cubicle offered little privacy. They stood no more than five-feet high, with two inches of plywood and fabric separating us from the next station. It didn't matter. Each of the bordering cubicles had its own world crisis to attend to. We would not be listened to, watched, or otherwise intruded upon.

"Let me begin by saying I think it's terrible what's going on in your homeland and I hope we'll see a swift, peaceful resolution before long."

The homeland in question was a mineral-rich pimple of a breakaway province that used to be safely tucked away behind the iron curtain. It hadn't known what to do with itself since the wall came down. Bloody civil war spiced with a generous dose of ethnic cleansing proved to be its new favourite pastime.

"Thank you," she replied. Her English was accented but solid. The press would like that.

"You're from a town, thirty miles outside the capital. Krez… Kro…"

I shuffled some papers looking for the specifics, but I didn't hunt too hard. The precise details weren't so important. She offered a pronunciation I couldn't hope to repeat, so I simply nodded. I might have asked her to spell it for the record, but she probably would have come back at me with something in Cyrillic.

"I understand you're one of the staff at the hospital there."

"I am."

"You work in the nursery?"

"No, I am with the cleaning crew."

"What do you clean?"

"Floors, walls, toilets."

"They have these things in the nursery?"

"Of course."

"So you've mopped the floor in there before? Scrubbed the walls, the toilets?"

"Of course."

"Then you work in the nursery."

"I supposed you could say so."

"I'm only repeating what you've told me yourself," I informed her.

I ticked off the first item on my checklist. Five or six questions to establish key facts was about average.

"It says here that armed militia entered your hospital yesterday morning."

"That is true."

"They were armed with bayonets, correct?"

"No."

"Did they have guns?"

"Yes."

"Did they have knives?"

"Yes."

"Then they had bayonets."

One plus one is two. Simple equation. She argued it anyway.

"The guns were not rifles, the knives they wore on their belts."

"Are you an arms expert?"

"No."

"Then they were armed with bayonets."

"All right," she agreed, not appreciating what an important detail this was. Now that it was established, I ticked it off on my list.

"Do you know why they came to the hospital?"

"They were there for a man who had been injured in a bombing. They asked for him by name at the front desk and went to his room."

"To kill him?"

"No. He was detained and taken away in a car."

"To be killed?"

"I have no idea. I did not see what became of him."

It didn't really matter. It wasn't on the checklist. The fate of one random bombing victim can't buy me any mileage. As far as anyone knew, it was a bomb he himself was working on that went off in his face. Guys like him don't sway public opinion, don't pull on heart strings. The sympathy factor wasn't there, the empathy-generation capacity was nil. Sometimes it pays to ask a question that doesn't cut to the chase, but Mr. Anonymous Bombing Victim was a dead end.

"Tell me who these men harmed at the hospital."

She shrugged, confused. "No one."

"You know this for certain?"

"Yes."

"So a squad of militia, armed with bayonets, march into a civilian hospital—they go in, they come out, and nobody gets hurt?"

"Yes."

"You were with them the whole time? You had your eye on each of them as they went from room to room?"

"No, I could not possibly…"

"So you can't account for their whereabouts or activities the whole time they were inside the hospital."

"I suppose not."

I nodded. That was worth a tick on the list.

Time was a factor. We had four senators, three congressmen, and at least a dozen ministers from various parliamentary democracies on hold. They were all waiting for us to feed them reasons for the moral outrage they were building to a fever pitch in preparation for their next appearance on the floor.

"How many entered the nursery?"

"None."

"You were in the nursery at the time?"

"No, I was on the ground floor."

"So then the answer is, you don't know."

It seemed like she was starting to understand how this worked.

"I don't know," she agreed.

"As far as you know, it could have been ten. A dozen. Twenty."

"Twenty men did not enter the nursery."

"How can you be so sure?"

"There were not twenty men in total."

"Okay," I conceded. "So we've established that not more than twenty armed men entered the nursery while you were lucky enough to be away from your post."

"We have?"

"That's what I see here," I said, making another careful tick.

I reviewed the facts on my checklist. There weren't many, but I took my time. The longer I stared at my paperwork, the more importance it took on, the more weight it seemed to carry. I continued when I felt my witness was suitably impressed by my careful contemplation of her meagre file.

"I just want to make sure I have the correct figures written down. Everybody wants to be accurate when we're talking about something so terrible."

The interview subject shook her head slowly in apparent agreement.

"How many newborns are typically in the nursery at your hospital?"

"The number varies. Sometimes greatly. We can have as few as two or three. Usually there are about ten. Our capacity is thirty."

"And how many babies were there in the nursery after the militia paid their visit to your hospital?"

"We had five. Three boys and two girls."

"So you're telling me that we're looking at as many as two dozen or more babies mercilessly bayoneted as they lay sleeping in their cribs."

"This is not what I am telling you at all. Before the men came, we had only…"

"How many babies were in the nursery before this war crime happened is immaterial. It's how many were left after that's important. I'm sure you agree. Our concern must now be for the survivors. The two dozen poor unfortunates are beyond our help."

"But there was no blood. No bodies…"

"Who knows what these monsters did with their little bodies," I said. "Does your hospital have an incinerator for biological waste?"

"We do, but they could not have…"

"I know. It's shocking what men can do in times of war. Try not to dwell on it. There was nothing you could have done to stop them."

I made a few final ticks and notes on the form and closed the file folder. I offered my witness a separate piece of paper written in a language she couldn't read and asked her to sign it. A legal formality.

"One of my associates will take you to our studio and ask you to repeat some of your testimony for the cameras. Try to keep to the facts as we've established them."

"But I am not certain of these facts."

"Rest assured, nothing you've told me comes as a surprise. It only corroborates what we already know. You see, we've had other reports of atrocities."

"From who?"

"Sources."

"What sources?"

"Our sources."

"But who are these sources?"

"Ordinary people just like you."

It seemed to reassure her. When the receptionist returned to collect her a moment later, she left with a look of patriotic fervour mixed into her sad eyes, confident she was doing a great service for her country.

She wasn't gone ten seconds before I had the front desk patch me through to the first senator's office. He was at the top of my need-to-know list and a line had been kept open. The House was in recess, but he would be next to take the floor and ride the lectern to political infamy once everyone was back. He was the one fate had chosen to break the story to the current news cycle.

When the senator got on the line, I made an effort to sound suitably grave.

"I'm afraid the situation has deteriorated, Senator. It's far worse than we could have imagined. We have an eyewitness report that the militia are breaking into hospitals and bayoneting babies."

"My God! I've never heard anything so horrible."

"Neither have I, Senator. Neither have I. We can only hope that enough impassioned speeches from our elected officials here and abroad can spur NATO into action."

He never questioned my report, assuming correctly that we had a signed affidavit and video testimony to back it up. In all my years at this job, not a single elected representative in any of the western democracies we service ever questioned one of my reports. They all know war is horrible, and babies getting bayonetted sounds like the sort of awful thing that might happen when a war breaks out. Particularly if that war involves an enemy state the current administration would like to bomb for various political and economic reasons. They don't specifically set out to lie to their own people. Not always. But they do go looking for confirmation—any confirmation—that this terrible thing they've imagined might be going on at the front lines. It doesn't take much of a search to find someone willing to claim, imply or otherwise invent an eyewitness account of these atrocities. Unsubstantiated reports, rumours and outright fabrications get quoted in firebrand speeches by political hacks fishing for support for their war, and public anger starts to snowball. How could it not? Picture all those poor babies.

On a brighter note, I wished the senator good fortune on the munitions contract he was trying to push through on behalf of his constituents. He was still a few votes short, but no one could ever predict when the world stage would offer up some new imperative for additional defence spending.

My phone rang the moment I was off with the senator.

"Call on line four," the receptionist told me.

"Who?"

She didn't dare say who.

I stood in my cubicle so I could see over all the dividing walls—all the way to the front desk. I caught the receptionist's eye. She looked back at me, still silent on the phone, and pointed straight up.

"Someone on seven?" I asked, wondering which suit wanted to bother me in the middle of my shift.

She shook her head no and stabbed her finger up into the air a few times. And then I knew what she meant. Way up. All the way to the top floor no one ever sees without a trip in a private elevator that needs a key, a card and a pass code.

I sat back down and punched the flashing button for line four immediately.

"Yes sir," I said, "How can I help you?"

"Are we solid on this little Euro-tussle?"

The voice was surprisingly robust for a man so old, but he did have the very best of everything money could buy to keep him going. The best doctors, the best medicine, the best replacement organs.

"The wheels are officially in motion," I told him. "A few more calls and all the balls will be in play."

"I want my futures position solid by the time our markets close so I can ride the wave on the Asian open."

The stock market always likes a war. And the more nations to pile in, the better. The nervous money would be on the way out right now. The smart money was buying. We'd be up triple digits starting tomorrow and again every day through the rest of the week.

"You'll make a killing, sir," I assured him.

"I always do," he said before the phone went dead.

● ● ●

My next appointment arrived shortly after I finished shocking my stable of politicians with graphic details that were old news to me, but fresh and horrific to all of them. Content that their moral outrage was fuelled for the next week of speeches and broadcast talking points, I focused on my other case. There was trouble brewing on another continent. A Catholic bishop stationed in central Africa had flown in on our dime and I had been assigned to speak to him. I saw him standing over the sea of cubicles, looking around, confused, until someone directed him to me.

Like every outsider who came to the sixth floor, he had little to no understanding of our operation. People look at our suite and think they see offices—paper pushers sitting at computer stations set up on IKEA desks, boxed inside blue cubicle walls, our skulls clamped in headsets and our asses clamped in swivel chairs. That's what they see, if they bother to look at all. If they looked closer, they'd see a factory floor with an assembly line working full steam all day every day. It's where we manufacture consent. We mass-produce it.

The bishop sat down across from me. I was disappointed he wasn't wearing robes or his tall, pointy hat. We'd have to remedy that for the press conference. Optics are just as important as the story that goes with them. Hopefully his official wardrobe ensemble was packed in his luggage. If not, I knew a costume outfitter who could probably set us up with something that looked authentic on short notice.

The problem the bishop presented was not the same kind I had just sorted out in Eastern Europe. His war had been going strong for nearly a full year and had long since dragged its neighbours and three former colonial powers into the conflict. Foreign troops were already stationed across the land as "peacekeepers" who were doing nothing of the sort. At this point, the murder and mayhem had dragged on for so long, support for the conflict was waning among the outside powers. This war needed a fresh jolt of energy if it was going to survive the peace negotiations that were threatening to bring it all grinding to a premature halt.

Eventually, like all tales of distasteful horror, even bayonetted babies lose their ability to shock and enrage over time. No matter how many fictional babies meet their end on the edge of a phantom blade wielded by a uniformed bugbear, such stories are only good for about a week or two worth of mass outrage before they grow old and lose their power to fill enlistment queues. So what are the propagandists and pundits and presidents to do to further inflame passion for war? What do they do to tip their people over the edge from initial fury, to full-fledged commitment to a long, costly and exceedingly bloody engagement?

They rape nuns.

"Tell me what happened at the convent, Your Holiness," I said.

The Last Seven Miles and Home

AS FAR AS I'M CONCERNED, it was his own fault. Sure, I'd been driving straight through the day and half the night, dead tired and wanting to get home fast, but I was in the lines. There's hardly any traffic at that time of night, out on those rural back roads, and you can hear a car coming from miles away. If you're hitching you get eager. Maybe too eager.

He was probably just as tired as me, plus cold and hungry on top of it. With his sign out, his thumb out, I would have seen him. Wouldn't have picked him up, but I would have seen him fine. He didn't have to go and stick his neck out, too.

Taking the turn, I saw my headlights sweep over him, too close to brake. I jerked the wheel to swerve, right instead of left. He had the same idea and tried to jump out of the way, back to the shoulder. We both chose wrong, otherwise I would have only clipped him at worst. As it was, he got hit straight on, mid-dive. The hood of my car buckled, but I never felt him go under the wheels.

I came skidding to a halt. Much farther and I would have rolled right off the side, hopped the ditch and landed in the brush. Then we'd have both been done, with no chance of anyone spotting us till morning. Small mercies.

I opened the door and got out straight away. No use sitting around in shock after an accident if you already know what happened and had a grip on it. I thought the impact might have punted the guy down the road thirty yards or so, but there was nothing sprawled on the pavement ahead. When I walked to the front of the car to see the damage for myself, I found him. He was embedded, lengthwise, into the grill. Only one of the headlights was still working and I wished he'd busted that one, too. All I could see by the light was the clump of bloody hair hanging across the spot where he used to have a face.

I could have called 911 then and there, and maybe I should have. But the hitcher was dead and my driver's licence was going to join him if I got any more demerits. I couldn't afford that, living out in the boonies, miles from work and anyplace else of note. Where I live, if you don't have a car to get around, you better be a mountain man living in a cabin in the woods. Hermits can get by without; everybody else commutes.

I looked around and there wasn't much to see. Trees, trees and more trees. But I knew the route, recognized the bend when I took it. I was only seven miles away from home and a warm bed. I'd never wanted to see my little house again quite so bad. It promised sleep, time to think, and a way to sort out this mess.

The hitcher's cardboard sign was out by the white line, slowly rotating in the breeze. "Anywhere but here," it said. It was then I decided to give him a ride after all.

There was no need to move the body. It was practically a part of the car, dug in as it was, with the bumper carrying him like a chrome platter. Stuck any deeper, he'd be in the engine block. The motor was still running and it sounded promising even with all the damage. There was no doubt my vehicle would still drive, no doubt he'd hang on till I got home, no doubt he'd still be just as dead when I got there. My only concern was whether anyone would spot us on the way.

I got back behind the wheel and all I needed to do was put the car in gear and ease forward. There was some scraping and complaining, but it rolled fine. I was back between the lines, finishing the turn I'd started ten minutes earlier, with an empty seat beside me but a passenger just the same.

I didn't have a full plan just yet, but I was working on it. In the car port, I could take my sweet time picking the body out of the grill, washing away all the blood, making sure I scraped out every last bit of gristle and thread of clothing. Once I was sure it was clean, spotless, I'd take the car in to the body shop for repairs and tell a tall tale about hitting a deer.

The hitcher would have to disappear, but that was simple enough. Home was a postage stamp of paved civilization, with cookie-cutter houses spread wide apart and dumped on a hundred and sixty acres of new development. There were trees out back, lots of them, damn near a forest, with plenty of land on my lot to call my own. The tree line would give me all the privacy I needed to dig. Deep enough so nothing that lives in the woods would ever claw the corpse out of the dirt, deep enough for me to one day forget all about this night. No one would ever know, so long as I never moved, never sold part of the property, never decided I wanted an in-ground swimming pool. Could I live with that? Sure. If I wanted a dip that bad, I could always hike to the lake.

The first mile was the worst. I could hear him, my stowaway, scraping away in the wheel wells. It wasn't the sound of metal and plastic, bent out of position, grinding against bits they weren't supposed to be attached to. This was organic. Flesh being peeled by friction, bone being worn down by the grindstone mechanics of a car just trying to get from Point A to Point B. It was a wet, sticky sound, and I spent a long time finding a late-night radio station with good enough reception to drown it out.

The road home took me through town. When I say "town" I mean a crossroad with a hardware store, a bank branch and a diner. There would be nobody around to see me pass through, everything would be closed, even the diner that stayed open late. Late in these parts amounted to 8:00 pm. This was why I moved out to the boonies. It's easy to be a private person when there are so few people to guard your privacy against.

I was almost at the final turn when I was stopped cold. The arm of a rail crossing swung down and blocked my way just as I was approaching. The road was narrow and the arm was long, but I considered gunning the car around it anyway to beat the train. A passenger express promised a lot of potential witnesses. Most of the riders would have been tucked in their sleepers, or dozing in their seats, but it only took one to be staring out the window at the darkness to spot the state of my car and its unusual hood ornament lit up by the red crossing lights. Would they understand what they were looking at? Would they mention it to somebody else? Report it to authorities?

The engine rumbled down the track and I waited to see if it was pulling discovery and jail for me. I spotted the engineer up at his controls, but all he cared to look at was the track ahead, making sure it was clear. His eyes were the sole ones I needed to concern myself with. It was only a freight, a mile long and slow, and I was happy for the rest it gave me from driving. It let me breathe again. My heart was back to a normal pace by the time the final hopper passed me by.

The tiny loop of side road was black when I got there. Hardly a single porch light was on, and no one had ever considered the expense of street lights worthwhile. I hit the button on the remote garage-door opener clipped to the driver-side sun visor in advance of my arrival. The door was up as I hit the driveway, and it was smooth sailing straight inside. The door swung back down behind me, and if the noise woke anybody curious enough to look out a window to see who'd just come home so late, it was shut before they could see a thing.

My bed was as warm as I'd hoped and sleep came easily when exhaustion trumped worries, guilt and doubt. I had made it, I was safe, and my troubles would be dealt with at my own pace.

It was past noon before I woke up, refreshed and ready to begin tackling the first round of clean-up. I didn't relish the job, and I fully expected my stomach to turn itself over a few times before it was done, but I'd gone hunting before. I'd helped clean a carcass. I didn't imagine this would be much worse. A spot of breakfast, a shower, and some old clothes I wouldn't mind burning once I was done, and I'd be ready to begin.

I was putting a kettle on when I spotted the first neighbour outside—lingering, watching, staring. I knew him from two houses down, but we'd never been friendly. I was wondering what he wanted when I saw another one come over and talk to him. There were more out there as well, standing in small groups, and they all had the same look on their face: concern.

I'd seen that look in well-meaning eyes before, when I was a kid and there had been a death in the family. It was the look of people who wanted to help and didn't know how, people who wanted to say something but couldn't think of anything better than small talk and common condolences. If I'd been the one to inspire such communal worry, I didn't understand why none of them had come to knock on my door yet.

And then I saw what had captured their attention. It was the red tire tracks. I could see the clear pattern of the treads from my window, etched all the way down the road. It was my hitchhiker who had forged the path. It seems he'd had seven miles worth of blood in him. Enough to paint my tires the whole way and mark a twin trail right up to my garage door. I couldn't see the dark blood on the blacktop by night. By day, I couldn't miss it. Neither could anybody else. The neighbours all saw it, had come for a closer look, and had collected out front. Eight years I'd been in that house and had never seen more than two of them at one time. Now they were all there, like I was throwing a housewarming party.

The final visitors to arrive were the police. No one even called them. All the highway patrol had to do was follow the trail I'd left for them.

The officers must have come directly from the scene of the accident after spotting the point of impact on the highway. Broken glass, broken teeth, a smear of burnt rubber, and blood. Lots of blood, with more of it pointing the way. I knew they'd been there because one of them had the cardboard sign in hand as he got out of the rover, the one with that longed-for destination scribbled in black marker: Anywhere but here.

That was a sentiment I had come to agree with.

It's the Thought
That Counts

IT WAS CHRISTMAS EVE and we were watching a live feed from the International Space Station where a special broadcast had been arranged by the National Aeronautics Space Agency. The news anchor was utterly deadpan as he gave his carefully worded introduction that stated there was a certain special someone who wanted to extend his Christmas greetings to children the world over. My little sister and I stared at the television in slack-jawed amazement as the satellite signal switched over to a live shot from within the station. The screen was instantly filled with a bright red suit and a cherubic face hidden behind a big white beard that floated gently in zero gravity. Santa Claus had made his first stop of the evening to give the astronauts their presents.

To a pair of dazzled kids, five and six years old, the footage had its desired effect, successfully mixing the magic of St. Nick and the space-age technology of the 21st century, giving the innocent children of a cynical world proof positive that the stories they'd heard about the jolly old elf were not invention, but solid fact. A Santa suit, brought aboard by a space-shuttle mission sent to resupply the station months earlier, had paid off with some good PR for NASA and a cute bumper for the six o'clock news on all the network affiliates.

That night, my sister and I went to bed buzzing with excitement, counting the minutes until morning, and waiting for sheer exhaustion to shepherd us into unconsciousness so the next day could come that much sooner.

My father came up to my room later that night as I lay tucked in my bed, still wide awake, anticipation eating away at me. His face was ashen.

"I'm sorry, son," he said. "Santa burned up on re-entry."

• • •

Father, for lack of a better word, was cheap. And gift-giving was something he saw as a senseless drain on both his time and his wallet. Throughout our childhood, he systematically killed off any and all mythological holiday icons in an attempt to balance the household budget.

The Easter Bunny was shot in a tragic hunting accident. Father took great pains to make the story authentic, keeping us informed day by day about his heroic struggle in the animal hospital as he lingered near death following multiple surgeries to remove all the buckshot. Inevitably, the bunny was overcome by his injuries, and a veterinarian had to be summoned to put him down by lethal injection just days before Easter. No chocolate eggs for us.

The Tooth Fairy fared no better when her majestic tooth castle, built from the baby teeth of countless generations of gummy children, collapsed due to faulty engineering, crushing her to paste under tons of molars and bicuspids. There were no quarters to be found under our pillows thereafter.

Cupid was felled by a volley of arrows when he foolishly crossed an archery range before the all-clear was sounded. Valentine's Day and all heart-shaped confectionaries died with him.

Even New Year's wasn't safe from the Grim Reaper. Although not an official gift-exchange day by any means, Father knew when he was on a roll and decided to do away with the mere annoyance of having to wish anyone a Happy New Year when he was trying to nurse a hangover. So, as the Old Year died a kidney-dialysis death in the geriatrics ward, Baby New Year, much to everyone's horror, became another statistic of Sudden Infant Death Syndrome.

Santa Claus's untimely demise on Christmas Eve, just hours before he was to deliver us our presents, was sad but hardly unexpected given the seasonal carnage we had become used to. We immediately realized there would be no chance of our parcels being recovered for this one final Christmas, as they had doubtless been incinerated in earth's upper atmosphere along with the Crispy Kringle and all nine of his tiny reindeer. Subsequent years saw the holiday still celebrated far and wide, but we knew it was all a sham—an elaborate hoax devised to spare the feelings of those naïve bumpkins who couldn't handle the truth of the tragedy that had befallen this most time-honoured of holidays. Christmas has been robbed of all meaning, save its most base religious connotations.

With nearly every gift -giving occasion obliterated from our calendar, Father's bank roll grew fat. There was only one other annual celebration to contend with, but it promised to be the biggest challenge to his murderous creativity. There were no fairies or elves to assassinate, no minions of mythology or anthropomorphic messengers of goodwill to declare dead. Birthdays simply had no figureheads to target. His solution, however, was simple.

A figurehead must be invented.

Laying the groundwork for this plan took several long years, during which my sister and I each enjoyed half-a-dozen pleasant birthdays, complete with presents, parties, and even a party clown. The clown was called Bobo, and as we grew older we got to be on a first-name basis with him. We could count on seeing Bobo the Clown twice a year because Father made sure to hire him for every one of our parties. Like clockwork, he would arrive in the afternoon to entertain a menagerie of screaming children with magic tricks, jokes and juggling, paying extra attention to the special birthday boy or girl. It wasn't long before Bobo became a tradition in our home.

Also a tradition was how we received our bounty of presents. They would always come with Bobo, tucked in the back of the little yellow hatchback he left parked by the curb. The birthday boy or girl would wait behind the front door, nose pressed to the bug screen, and watch as Bobo slogged up our path in his size twenty-two shoes, a bag of dazzlingly wrapped boxes, big and small, slung over his shoulder. He'd honk his shiny red nose as he arrived at the stoop and dumped his load on the porch. Like a shot, we'd be outside, tearing through the wrapping like a paper shredder. Rain or shine, every gift would be exposed to the open air before it ever crossed the threshold.

The highlight of each Bobo visit came towards the end of the party, when he would reveal the grand illusion of the day. This was always some elaborate magic trick he would have to assemble whenever there was clown downtime. As we ate cake or played a round of Pin the Tail on the Donkey, Bobo would work diligently with his Phillips screwdriver, assembling some fantastic masterwork of trickery to make our jaws drop and our tongues waggle. We never knew what it was until, late in the afternoon, we'd turn away from our game of tag or our efforts to beat a piñata to death blindfolded, and see the finished product ready for action.

Bobo's big prop was usually some sort of cabinet, colourfully painted with moons and stars and other designs meant to suggest the mystical. In it, he would perform some variation of what was essentially the same trick. But each time he ran through his routine, he mixed up the comedic interplay and the specifics of the illusion to convince all the kids present that they were seeing it for the first time. My sister, or I, or sometimes the two of us—being the guests of honour and the children of the host who was paying the shot—would be asked to function as Bobo's dutiful assistants. Following the clown's instructions to the letter, we would help him saw himself in half, or chop his head off with a play guillotine, or displace various body parts that would continue to wiggle or wave at us through strategically placed holes. Through it all, Bobo would mug for his hysterical audience, feigning fear, screaming in mock agony, pleading for mercy. And we would eat it up, squealing with delight as we followed his lead on how to mutilate him safely with a tap of a wand and the correct magic word. At the end of it all, Bobo would emerge from his cabinet or box intact to take his bows and accept the enthusiastic applause of every boy and girl in attendance.

As the years rolled by, the act became old and familiar, but remained the anticipated climax of every backyard birthday party. And despite a few occasions when the weather wasn't very cooperative, it always went off without a hitch.

Except for the year with the swords.

The swords weren't real swords. No knight of the realm would dare wield them in battle. Nevertheless, they were steel, they were quite heavy, and they were surprisingly sharp at the tip. We knew this because Bobo asked us to examine the swords carefully to confirm they were the genuine article and not some cardboard dupe. My sister and I both assured the audience that the swords were the real deal. We even clanged them together several times in a mock duel so everyone could hear the metallic ring.

Bobo squeezed himself into his cabinet that stood tall and narrow on our lawn. He shut the door and stuck his face out through the convenient hole that would allow us to see every funny face he made as the trick progressed. My sister and I fit our swords into the ready-made slots on either side of the cabinet. Both were angled downward towards vital areas of Bobo's unseen body, ready to deliver a mortal blow. Two more slots, opposite the entry points, yawned open to expose the sword tips once they had been thrust through the clown, concluding the illusion.

Bobo instructed us to start feeding the swords through the cabinet until their progress was halted by something solid.

"Oooo, that tickles!" Bobo giggled as the swords poked him in the ribs. All the children laughed at this.

"Something must be in the way. I can't imagine what!" he told us.

"You are!" the audience screamed in delight. "You're in the way," they all laughed.

"Okay kids," said Bobo, "I want you to give those swords a good hard push. Put your backs into it! Ready?"

My sister and I nodded and braced ourselves for the big push.

"On three!" Bobo said, and the whole audience yelled the countdown with him. "One...two...three!"

My sister and I put all our weight behind the thrust. There was a moment of resistance, but then the swords passed through the rest of the cabinet with surprising ease until the tips of the blades poked out the opposite sides for all to see.

Bobo didn't say "Ta-da!" like he usually did when he pulled off a successful magic trick. He only wheezed once and gurgled. Then he spat up some blood. More blood came pouring out of the sword exit holes, pooling in the grass, soiling our shoes. I was in shorts, and my legs were thoroughly spattered with chicken-pox blood stains. My sister's white summer dress was ruined.

The laughter of the children became screams. Bobo's eyes rolled back in his head. His body tried to collapse inside the cabinet, but the swords held him up. We had all been there on previous occasions to see the saw pass through his torso, the bed of nails perforate his back. This wasn't how the trick was scripted.

It was only after we'd been whisked inside to our rooms and the party evacuated by concerned parents in minivans that we realized what we had done. We had executed Bobo the Clown.

In the days that followed, Father, to his credit, did his best to assure us that it wasn't our fault. Obviously, Bobo the Clown had made some terrible miscalculation with the mechanics of his trick, leading to his untimely demise. My sister and I, however, remained inconsolable, and birthdays became dead to us. When the next birthday in our family arrived, it came and went unacknowledged. By the first anniversary of the Bobo incident, we had recovered enough to be able to say "Happy Birthday" aloud, but that was as festive as it ever got again. Birthdays, like Christmas and Easter and all the lesser occasions before and after and in-between, had become just another day on the calendar. And the concept of a "happy" birthday existed only in the traditional greeting we shared joylessly, as a means of formally adding a year to our ages.

From Father's point of view, the birthday party massacre had an unexpected bonus attached to it. Not only did it put an end to our own festivities, it got my sister and I promptly uninvited to all our friends' birthday parties as well. Father never had to buy us any more presents, and he didn't need to supply us with any token offering for anyone else either. The reason for our ostracization was clear enough to us. We imagined the other parents were concerned we might unwittingly impale someone and ruin their birthday celebrations as well. Hushed talk about a "sick trick" and an "unfit father" never registered in our minds as being connected with the Bobo the Clown manslaughter case we were so relieved never made the papers.

I was nearly twelve years old, in the last term of my final year of grade school, when the truth surfaced at last. There was a new crossing guard guiding us across the busiest street of the school zone. Months went by and I never looked at him twice, until the one time in the spring semester I got a detention designed to teach me a lesson I can't remember for doing something bad I can no longer recall. Hurrying home late, I arrived at the crosswalk in time to see our guard heading home for the day. He was a block away, letting himself into his parked car. It was a little yellow hatchback that I would never have associated with anything in particular until I saw the familiar body type with an unmistakable gait stroll up to it. That's when I knew Bobo the Clown lived.

I walked up to the car in a trance and stopped in front of the driver's side window, staring at my unwitting crime, freshly risen from the grave. He wore no red nose, his face wasn't made up, and I noted his shoes were sensible loafers, no bigger than size ten at most. Nevertheless his other facial features leapt out at me. They had been burned into my brain by that last horrible glimpse years before, as his eyes rolled back and blood streamed out of his mouth.

The crossing guard, still picking through his keys, noticed me standing next to his car, eyes bugged, mouth agape. He rolled down his window and asked, with no glimmer of recognition, "Yeah?"

"Bobo," I said to him, not a question but a simple surprised statement. Perhaps if I had added a question mark to my tone, it would have given him the opportunity to deny any knowledge of this Bobo person and retreat before anything else could be asked. As stated, however, he was pinned to the spot like an escaped convict caught in a guard-tower searchlight.

Maybe it was the guilt or a need to come clean, but once he recognized me—somewhat older, somewhat matured, yet still the same wounded boy from the world's worst birthday party—there was only one thing he could think to say.

"Get in."

I hurried around to the passenger side. My father had warned us about talking to strangers, had insisted we never get into a car with anybody we didn't know. But this was Bobo, and I knew him as well as any grown man I'd ever met. I had, after all, murdered him.

Twenty minutes later, we were sitting together in a burger joint. I was having a milkshake, his treat. After the barest minimum of pleasantries and small talk, he unloaded his conscience. It was a tale of heartache and alimony, details of which had been pried loose by my father each time he was hired for a new party. Apparently, Father timed his offer carefully to coincide with the lowest point in Bobo's personal finances and misery. In a moment of weakness, he'd agreed to the insidious plot.

"He made it worth my while," said Bobo the Clown-cum-Crossing Guard. "Five grand for the stunt and hush money."

I was still too young to have much money sense, but I knew for sure that five thousand dollars buys a lot of birthday presents. Years' and years' worth.

Bobo could see the shock on my face when he told me the figure.

"Yeah, it didn't come cheap. I knew I'd have to retire Bobo the Clown after that and invent a whole new character. That meant a new makeup design and new business cards. I had to build my rep from scratch."

He ran through a tainted résumé that read like the sorry results of a gypsy hex. Bobo had worked under a number of guises and pseudonyms since the days of his preferred nom-de-plume. For a time he was Bibi the Clown, then BooBoo. He tried establishing himself as BamBam, Bonzo, Benny, and Banana. Nothing seemed to work. Convinced that the B-names were somehow cursed, he tried being Tinkle the Clown for a short time, but with no better luck. It didn't matter how far out of town he tried to peddle his services, eventually it came out that he was the party clown implicated in the conspiracy to traumatize a partyload of children. The phone stopped ringing, circulars and fliers refused to carry his advertisements, and the police kept a close eye on him. Bobo loved children, but his one malicious and well-paid-for transgression had destroyed his means of entertaining them. All conceivable avenues became blocked, and Bobo found himself blacklisted when he sought employment as a daycare worker, a candy striper, a summer-camp counsellor and an ice-cream truck driver. Eventually he had to resort to a job that required no background check whatsoever and became a crossing guard. For as much as ten seconds at a time, he could be with children as they crossed a busy road under the protective shield of his plastic stop sign. For these brief moments Bobo knew happiness again, though he was always very careful to never be the least bit amusing. He remained ever fearful that if he were caught entertaining children between one sidewalk corner and the next, it would cost him his job.

My late afternoon milkshake binge with Bobo weighed heavily on me. The horrible deceit of his faked death was, I suspected, only the tip of iceberg. Later that week, after I had sufficiently recovered from the initial shock, I turned to the public library archives to confirm the rest of the lies. How many more untimely deaths had been a fabrication? In turn I looked up each and every person or entity my father had declared deceased over the years. Only the car accident that had claimed Mother when I was quite young proved to be legitimate. The rest, though they each had only a dubious claim to reality in the first place, proved to be very much alive in a manner of speaking. At least none of them had been pronounced dead. The library contained no tell-all books about St. Nick published to cash in on the legal inability to libel the dead. Old yellowing tabloids failed to produce a single death-watch front page detailing the brave final days of the Easter Bunny. Even the obituaries, going back years on carefully archived microfiche, seemed steadfastly determined to only eulogize real people— not dentally obsessed fairies and elves, holly or jolly.

After conferring with my sister at length about my findings, we agreed on a plan to force our father to admit his deception. Operating as an efficient tag team, we worked in shifts, ceaselessly nagging Father to take us on a road trip. It was no vacation destination park—amusement, national or theme—we wished to see. We wanted to go to a cemetery and we made the request at ten minute intervals every waking hour of the day, layering on as much whining as we thought necessary to drive Father mad. We remained so guilt-ridden about Bobo's horrific death, we told him, that we felt it was only proper we visit his grave to pay our respects. Father was taken aback by our sudden unquenchable thirst to see a final resting place that didn't exist, and we felt it was only a matter of time and a few thousand more tearful high-pitched tantrums before he would be forced to admit there was no such clown grave in existence.

Following weeks of pestering, our voluminous whines were suddenly silenced one day when Father caught us completely unawares and agreed to drive us to Bobo's grave. My sister and I held back on our usual rowdy car-trip banter. Instead we sat silently, stoically, like well-behaved children. In truth, we were deeply apprehensive. We knew this was some final desperate gambit on Father's part, and neither of us dared guess how far he was willing to take it in his effort to get us to drop the subject of Bobo's untimely demise.

The drive took us far from our suburban home, out into the countryside, through half a dozen tiny rural communities and much farmland. I figured Father's plan was to drive us around until we grew bored and begged him to turn back for home, or at least a rest stop. We responded with more silence and no demands.

Just when I was sure Father would be the first to give in and admit we were on a long trip to nowhere to pay our respects to nothing at all, he pulled the car over to the side of the dirt road we'd been on for nearly half an hour.

"We're here," he said simply and got out of the car.

My sister and I didn't move. Instead, we watched our father hop over the shallow drainage ditch next to the road and wade through the rows of bulrushes to the field beyond. He didn't wait for us and he didn't look back. My sister glanced my way, uncertain whether to laugh or cry, seeking some sign from me. I unbuckled my seatbelt and opened the door on my side of the back seat. She followed my lead. Together, we quickly caught up with Father as he crested a hill and arrived at a rusty iron fence.

The fence cordoned off a small square of forgotten country real estate containing no more than a couple dozen graves marked by stones of various sizes. The stones were weathered white, smoothed to the point where it was difficult to read the original inscriptions. Father made no attempt to enter the cemetery. Nobody had been buried there in at least a century and the grounds were neglected and forgotten. Instead, he walked along the length of the fence and into the wooded area well behind the graves. We were going to a special clown cemetery, he told us, far off the beaten path.

When it seemed possible we might actually be visiting a real grave, my sister stopped to pick some wild flowers. A humble offering for Bobo, who she wasn't certain was dead or alive at this point.

Deep in the woods, well removed from the road or any other signs of civilization, we came across a slight clearing, wide enough to let a few beams of sunlight in from the cluster of branches overhead.

And there was indeed a grave waiting for us. A pristine marble tombstone, fresh from the mason's, was set in place at the head of a six-foot-long patch of disturbed soil. Chiseled into its face in bold letters was one word: "Bobo."

Tears rolled down my sister's face as she set her improvised bouquet down on the grave. It was too much for me.

"It's a lie!" I yelled at Father. "Bobo's not dead! I know it's all a lie!"

I never thought I could be so forward with my accusations against Father, but the tombstone pushed me over the edge. In it, I saw the price of so many simple gifts he could have bought for us to mark the special dates of our childhood instead of investing in this absurd and expensive ruse.

"Dig," he commanded. "Dig if you don't believe me."

He reached behind a tree and retrieved a muddy spade that had been too-conveniently left there. Recently so. Other than the dried earth encrusting it, it looked new and still had a barcode sticker on the handle. Father threw it to the ground next to the grave and challenged me again with a withering glare.

We'd all come too far for me to back down now. I was determined to call his bluff. Defiantly, I picked up the shovel and stabbed it into the mound of dirt. The next two hours were hard going, but with puberty looming, I'd started to put on some new muscle that allowed me to progress through the gruelling entrenchment. The sun was beginning to set when I struck solid wood. I fell over at the bottom of the deep hole I'd dug, I was so surprised. I hadn't expected to find anything at all except blisters and a grudging admission of guilt from my father.

I looked up at him. Father towered over me, perched at the lip of the grave. He said nothing, but raised his eyebrows at me expectantly.

I began to unearth the smooth wooden lid of the casket that lay buried at the bottom of the hole. I recognized what it must be from my memories of the funeral home display room. There had been many to choose from when Mother died. I remembered the sullen funeral director congratulating Father on his tasteful choice from what he called "the lower end of the spectrum." This casket was much nicer. Even half-buried, the quality of the wood, the finish, and the ornate brass handles was obvious. Judging by its superb condition, I wouldn't have guessed it had been in the ground very long at all.

Again I looked up at Father on his grim perch. He responded with a single nod, daring me to go all the way, questioning whether I was brave enough to take a look inside his soil-wrapped present.

The drive home was just as silent as it had been coming down. I didn't sit in the back next to my sister. Instead, caked head to toe in mud, I buckled myself into the front passenger seat, where the dirt might be easier to vacuum off the upholstery.

Father didn't speak because there was no need to rub in what he saw as his final vindication. Bobo had been laid to rest in his grave, just as he'd promised us. I had stabbed the spade into the side of the coffin and pried up the lid no one had bothered to screw shut to see for myself. His corpse looked remarkably well preserved for someone who had been dead several years. The sword wounds in his clown suit were just as remarkably fresh. Only the grease paint was different than I remembered, as if applied by someone unfamiliar with the precise technique and design. This, suggested my sister as she peered down into the hole, might have been a trick of the fading daylight, or a distortion caused by Bobo's final death agony. I agreed that could explain the unusual configuration of his makeup, as well as the ugly bruising on his neck at the base of his skull.

Taking pity on my swollen, blistering fingers, Father resealed the coffin himself and filled in the grave again before we all walked back to the car.

"Was that really Bobo?" my sister whispered to me when Father was well ahead of us and out of earshot.

"Yeah," I told her.

"So we really did kill him after all?"

"Somebody sure did," was the only answer I gave her.

From that day forward we often, silently, questioned Father's truthfulness. But we never again questioned his sincerity.

Just One of the Lads

I'LL THANK YOU not to talk to me about "real man" sports. You can take your rugby, your hockey, and your football, American and Australian. I've no time for any of it, either playing or watching. There's no spark nor soul to it anymore, and if you're tuned in for the violence, you'd might as well turn on some boxing and watch a couple of big black buggers punch the crap out of each other. But even that's more dancing than beating, and they ruined the sport the day they started wearing gloves.

My game is darts. Not the usual bit of turns tossing pins into cork, but how me and the lads used to play it down Lembiegh way, at Charlie's pub round the corner the shops. The rules were the same, or reasonably so, but we added a personal human touch to the proceedings. His name was Ernie Kozak.

Ernie was older than any of us what came to drink at Charlie's—even older than Charlie himself who was old enough to be any of our fathers (and might have been in some cases). We figured Ernie in his mid-fifties, but no one ever asked him to confirm it. Ernie had a spot of deafness and probably couldn't read much beyond the brand name on a bottle of lager, so there was no getting through to him. Even if we could, it'd be a hell of a time understanding whatever it was he had to say back at us. His lips couldn't form the words, and the only time he made any noise beyond breathing was when we had a sing along and he moaned to the tune he felt vibrating through his bones.

Ernie had a mild case of elephantiasis that ran all through his head and down his right arm. His skin was thick and lumpy in these places, and felt like a life's worth of work calluses. He was always at Charlie's, from opening to closing, and he was always there for us when we fancied a round of darts.

Charlie's pub had a regular regulation board nailed to the wall in back, but no one ever much used it. Come a real round, we'd play together up front with the whole crowd to watch. At the start of the game, we'd send one of the lads to collect Ernie from his stool at the bar. Whoever was chosen would tell Ernie why he was needed, even though he couldn't have heard a word. It wasn't a matter anyways, since he was only ever called upon for one thing. He'd get up straight away and walk to the wall as everyone cheered him on and patted him on the back. Ernie was a darts man if ever there was one, and playing the game made him one of the gang.

Once the crowd had settled and the dart sets were chosen by the players, we'd position Ernie. He'd stand with his back to the wall and face forward. Lined up straight, he was the perfect height and size. At the tourney's commencement, he'd bring his malformed hand up to his face and cover his eyes, palm facing out. His mouth would shut tight, and the first volley would be thrown into his face.

The scoring for head darts had to be different from regular darts because of the difference in playing fields. When we'd first started playing with Ernie, some of us had tried painting numbers on him. It never looked right though, and half the time we'd forget to bring any paint anyways, so we started scoring by features. For doubling in and out, we had to strike his ears. That was a tricky shot from the front, but they stuck out enough for us to manage. His fingers, from pinky to index, were valued in increments of five, and his thumb was worth triple of whatever the last scoring dart was. Anywhere else on his face was worth a basic ten, except for his nose, the tip of which was the bull's eye.

Now those of you who were never there and never saw this game are liable to be judgmental. But I'll tell you straight off that we never threw the darts at Ernie hard. We just tossed them. Half the time they didn't stick into his skin at all, but we'd count the point anyway so as we wouldn't have to throw any more darts at Ernie than necessary. And even when they did stick, it wasn't like it hurt him or anything. He'd breathe a little harder when one hit—you could hear the air whistle through his nose faster—but that was probably just because he was excited. He loved playing darts with us. And his skin was so thick, he could take darts all night long and never shed a single drop of blood. Except when one hit him on his pinky finger. He wasn't too lumpy there, so it would bleed a bit sometimes. But it was only worth five points, so no one aimed for it much.

Once the game was over, we'd all chip in to buy Ernie a few pints and he'd go back to his stool and nurse them for the rest of the evening. This would happen three or four times a week, and always on Friday nights and Saturdays when we were off, so Ernie did pretty well for himself. At least, he went on fine for years until the landlords started developing our neighbourhood. New people were moving in, trying to be neighbourly, and of course coming down to the pub for a social spot or two.

The week they started coming into Charlie's we didn't play any darts at all, which I think upset Ernie the most because he had to buy his own drafts for the first time in ages. But the lot who came in seemed decent folk, so we picked up with the games again soon enough. We knew we weren't up to anything wrong or illegal, but you never know how outsiders are going to react to certain local customs. You know how it is, I'm sure. But like I said, they were a decent bunch, and they really got a kick out of the game when they saw it for themselves. That first night we even let one of them toss a few into Ernie's head to show him it wasn't some trick. Ernie was so pleased he was back on the wall that he forgot to close his mouth for smiling so much. Nearly got a yellow-feathered dart down his throat, but luckily his lip stopped it at the last moment.

We figured things would be fine from then on, but word got around to all the latest additions to the local population, and you won't be surprised to hear some of them thought it was "just awful." It was mostly the women who came down to the pub to complain and shout at us about what we were doing to "poor old Ernie." They never caught us during a match, but it was at those times that I wished Ernie could speak up and tell them to piss off and that he was having a fine time with his buddies down at Charlie's.

Anyway, it wasn't long before the complaints got official in tone, and Jerry Connoly had to come down during the day and in uniform to tell Charlie he'd better put a stop to the matches or there would be trouble. Jerry'd been known to toss a few at Ernie in his time, but we knew he was the law and it was only his job to come tell us. We preferred to hear it from him than someone else.

So that was the end of the head-darts matches at Charlie's. In many ways I suppose it was just as well. Some of the new residents were wanting to get in on the games, and they just weren't as careful as we were about tossing into Ernie's face only. He wasn't as well packed beyond his head and arm, and a shot to his neck or chest might have really hurt him apart from scoring a naught.

Ernie still hung around from opening till closing like he always did, but he never got to play darts with us again. Some of us used the dart board in back, but not nearly as often as we'd used Ernie. A few of the lads even invited Ernie to play in back with them one time, but they had a hell of a time explaining what they wanted from him. At first he just stood up against the wall, in front of the dart board, and took his old position. They finally got it into his head that they wanted him to throw darts with them. But Ernie didn't take to that idea too well and just wandered back to his stool up front and faded into the background. It was a dumb idea anyway. It's not like he could have thrown very well at all, what with the pulpy mess his right hand was.

I moved to a different town not so long after, and I can't say I want to rush back to see anyone soon. Lembiegh is a dull little village with damn little to do. But I still think of old Ernie sometimes, standing there with a dart or two hanging out of his face and smiling between rounds. I suppose he still goes to Charlie's, not like there's much else for him to do. And I guess some of the lads still buy him a round for old time's sake. But for the most part I bet he keeps to himself and buys his own drinks now with whatever the government pays him for being what he is. His days of glory may be gone, but he still has the same crowd of friends all around him. I wonder if he's happy.

Black Ink

"I CAN'T DO THAT ONE FOR YOU," I told the kid. "Pick something else."

He'd been in my shop before. Just looking. Now he'd stopped looking. He'd made his decision, he was old enough to get his first, and I was the artist he wanted.

"What's the sign say?" he asked, pointing up at the one over the door.

Any tattoo. Your choice.

I didn't have to look. I knew what the sign said. I wrote that sign myself. Letter by letter in fancy script. The fanciest I knew how, just to show off my skill. My talent.

"The sign's wrong," I said.

"I seen some of the swastikas you done for bikers," the kid told me.

"The swastika is an ancient symbol of good luck in certain cultures."

Standard response for anyone who asks or comments. I do designs, I do words, I don't do meaning. The customer can decide what it means. Me, I don't care.

"That's serious Neo-Nazi shit is what that is. Why you do that for them and not this for me?"

"Because the Gestapo isn't going to beat my ass for stealing their material. The Russian mob will."

What the kid wanted was something he'd found in a book about the Russian mafia. To him, it was just a badass design. To me it was trouble. Eastern European gangsters are touchy about their ink. Every tattoo—and there's hundreds of them—means something specific. It's the story of their lives, it's their criminal record. One look at the body of another man in their trade and they know everything there is to know about him. This isn't fashion for them, it's stigmata.

"If any of them sees you wearing one of their tats and they know you didn't earn it, they'll kill you. They'll cut it right off your body and before they kill you, they're going to make you tell them who gave it to you. And then they'll come and kill me too."

"Get something else," I damn near pleaded. "Anything else. A fucking heart with 'Mother' on it for all I care. Whatever. But not that."

"Pussy," he said. It was an insult directed at me, but it would probably be the same label stuck on him once his friends found out he didn't get the design he said he would.

"Don't be like that. I'll give you a piercing instead if you want. On the house. Just don't tell anyone I did it for free."

"What's the most expensive piercing you do?" he asked, and I could tell he was tempted.

I considered lying, but what was the point? There was another sign over my shoulder with all the options and prices posted.

"Cocks," I said. "Cocks go for five hundred bucks."

I hate doing cocks, but five c-notes and rubber gloves go a long way.

"I never thought about getting a cock ring before," he considered thoughtfully. "You think Shannon will like it?"

I hear his girl, Shannon, didn't like the new pierced cock with the ring so much. I also hear he ran through four other girls who liked it a lot better right after she left, so I guess it worked out for him.

Pierced or not, the kid was still hung up on that damn tattoo he'd set his heart on. He found someone else to give him what he wanted three weeks later. One week after that, he was dead. Nobody knows who killed him, but his freshly minted tat was skinned off him before the swelling even had time to go down. Word is the one with the knife asked him who had done his ink for him. They asked and he told. And they didn't have to slice off the tattoo to get him to talk. They pulled his cock ring out first. Then they peeled him.

Twenty years I've been in this business. Mick had only been inking for ten. He was good, very good. Skilled. But one day he gave a stupid kid the wrong tattoo and now there's less competition in town.

Talent doesn't count for shit if you don't know when not to use it.

Anatomy of a Riot

Eccleston University
April 11, 1846
6:03 am

"OSWALD, WANT TO SEE SOMETHING FUNNY?"

"Not at this time of day," said the first-year medical student who had been up half the night and under the covers for no more than three hours.

"But you must!" insisted his roommate, Clark, who had been up almost as late and had accomplished far more mischief. "Hurry, before it's too late."

"How funny is it?" asked Oswald, unprepared to commit to opening his eyes just yet.

"It is," Clark claimed in all sincerity, "hilarious."

● ● ●

This unfortunate incident began, as many unfortunate incidents do, with a raised hand. Whether they be hands raised to volunteer, hands raised to direct a pointed question at a lectern, or hands raised while making a solemn oath, too often no good comes of it. This hand, however, had been raised without the consent of the owner, who was past all questions and oaths at that point. He had certainly volunteered for something once, but not this.

• • •

"See it?" said Clark, who had steered Oswald to their third-floor window.

It took a moment for Oswald to focus, for his eyes to adjust to the morning sunlight outside, but when he directed his gaze to the tall elm tree opposite their quarters, he couldn't help but see. Buds were on the tree, but it was too early in the season for leaves. As such, the hand hung entirely exposed and unmistakable, high over the stone path that encircled the main buildings of the campus. It was a human hand, and a good portion of the forearm, cleanly severed before the elbow. It was clinging to one of the lower branches in an apparent death grip but, in reality, hung there more like an ornament.

Clark cackled, "Poor bastard should've held on tighter!"

"Take it down," groaned Oswald.

"Why? I wasn't the one who put it up there."

"I don't care. Take it down before someone sees."

• • •

Not one person had seen the hand dangling from the tree branch at that early hour. In fact, it was several people who had seen it, three in total. Together they had returned to town to report what they had witnessed up at the university while they were delivering a dozen flanks of ham to the kitchen, earmarked to feed students and staff alike come supper. Had they gone directly to the police to complain, tragedy might have been averted. The pranksters in question would have been officially admonished, suspended and perhaps even expelled, and the shameful event would have been hushed up and forgotten in short order. Alas, the butcher's delivery men and one kitchen cook instead chose to tell their tale to less prudent ears.

The Triple Mast Tavern
April 11, 1846
7:45 am

"It was body parts, I say! Arms and legs and even a head," declared Winston to an enthralled audience of ten.

It was too early for anyone to be drinking at The Triple Mast, but a few morning callers had arrived to gossip, to have a bite to eat. And, of course, there were also those who had failed to go home at all the previous night.

"I only saw a hand. One hand," said Langdon, who had worked in the university kitchen for five years and was less inclined to slander the alma mater that paid his wages. Nevertheless, he was compelled to back up the story of the campus tree adorned with human remains.

The other delivery man, Sommers, known for his honesty and disdain for tall tales and exaggeration, merely nodded in agreement. Winston was prone to run off at the mouth, but Sommers was willing to back at least part of his account. He, too, had only spotted one hand in the tree. There may have been more, he couldn't say for sure. But as far as he was concerned, one was as bad as twenty. It was sacrilege, an indignity, and it confirmed the worst of the rumours he'd ever heard of what the medical students got up to after class.

"Studies, they call it. Desecration is what it is," declared one of the audience.

"They're robbing graves up there! Stealing our own dead out from under us. And for what?" asked another.

"Unholy experiments," came the answer quick enough.

"Chops 'em up to all bits and pieces, I heard. Like dog food."

"They eat the best bits! I know it! Lot of cannibals, they are."

The two men from the butcher shop said nothing to counter this. They made regular deliveries of beef, pork and fowl to the university. Surely enough to feed everyone there. Surely more than enough to keep them from resorting to cannibalism. But the conversation had taken on a life of its own and left their initial report of the wayward hand far behind now.

● ● ●

By the mid 1800s, grave robbing for medical purposes had gone out of vogue. By that point, anatomists and doctors-in-training had little need to turn to the black market to procure the cadavers they needed for study. Private donations of corpses were arranged through families and lawyers, usually with the pre-mortem consent of the subject himself. The value of performing autopsies and dissections on human remains was no longer questioned among educated men. Improvements in medical science were becoming obvious, even to the layman, and visits from a doctor were increasingly cause for hope rather than dread. The speed at which the medical profession was advancing was unparalleled in human history, and thanks to the legalized examination of human remains, medicine had leapt forward from hocus-pocus conjecture to reliably provable treatments. The days of leeching and the balancing of the four humours was vanishing in favour of accurate diagnoses and medicinal applications that would come to benefit all of humanity.

Of course, there were still those, staggering in their numbers, who would have none of it.

Eccleston University
April 11, 1846
8:10 am

"Did you take care of that thing?" asked Oswald, encountering Clark in the hallway after he'd gotten dressed and gathered his texts.

"What thing?" replied Clark.

"The thing we discussed earlier."

"Oh that. Yes, quite handled I should say."

Oswald ignored the distasteful pun.

"And nobody saw you?"

"Nobody who counts," Clark ensured him, but Oswald still looked concerned.

"Admit it," said Clark, "it was funnier than Brent's foot-in-the-boot or that eye-on-rye last semester."

"They were all childish and stupid tricks," Oswald scolded, even as he failed to contain a slight smile. "But none of them could outdo the time Petersen rigged that cadaver to sit up in the middle of class."

"That," agreed Clark, "was classic."

● ● ●

A ladder had been procured, the hand taken down and returned to its appropriate drawer in the surgical theatre. None of the professors had witnessed the prank, and only a handful of students had the opportunity to appreciate the high jinx, largely fuelled by alcohol, that had developed over the previous night. No harm, they thought, had been done, other than the obvious indignity to a body—or at least a small portion of a body. It was not the first time medical students had pressed a cadaver or its limbs into inappropriate service for the sake of the joke, nor would it be the last. But such gallows humour was typically overlooked or only mildly reprimanded. These acts of seemingly callous indifference to mortality and the final wishes of those who had generously offered their remains for the betterment of scientific understanding were often merely a coping mechanism for young men who were looking death in the face for the first time in their lives. If they could not poke fun at death's expense, and took their work and studies too seriously, there was a very real danger of them becoming unhinged. Every professor had seen it before, both as a teacher and during their own days as students. It was best, they concluded, to mete out punishment in the form of extra duties and longer hours rather than expulsions whenever possible.

For those who sought to wield any control over death, the first empowering step was to learn how to laugh at it.

The Triple Mast Tavern
April 11, 1846
8:37 am

Word of the heated discussion going on at The Triple
Mast had leaked out, and the place was quickly filled
with other concerned and affronted citizens who
shared a low opinion of the medical shenanigans they
suspected were going on at the university.

"We should go up there and give them what for!"
was the inevitable suggestion cried out over the
murmur and fuss of the tavern.

A roar of agreement grew, attracting more attention from passersby outside who poked their heads in
to see what was at issue. Before long, The Triple Mast
was bursting at the seams and the gathering had no
choice but to start spilling into the street. Once the
flood of angered humanity came pouring out the door,
there was little holding it back from becoming a mob
in flow. Collectively, they decided to begin their march
on Eccleston University, egging on stragglers and
picking up more numbers on the way.

It was a long hike up to the campus, with no horse
or cart to carry any of them, but the mob was a self-
fuelling source of energy, and so long as the anger
went unanswered, the crowd spurred itself and moved
as one.

● ● ●

The so-called "Anatomy Riots" of the late 17th and early 18th centuries were a reoccurring phenomenon across New England. They cropped up at regular intervals here and there, usually at medical universities, and lasted nearly a century as humanity bridged the gap from fear and superstition to an age of reason and science. The mistreatment of bodies, suspected or witnessed, was typically the cause, as well as accusations, mostly false, of graverobbing, body snatching and desecration.

Such riots continued to happen until the practice of body donation was almost universally accepted by the law and the public of states, provinces and territories across the continent. It was a long process, and outrage over what might be happening to human corpses behind closed doors, in lecture halls and mortuaries, ultimately led to a great deal of other fresh corpses adding to their number.

Eccleston University
April 11, 1846
11:50 am

A small dinner was served to the students daily between morning classes and afternoon studies. The dining hall could be relied upon to fill quickly with those seeking food and social interaction as soon as the bell was rung.

"Did everybody get a chance to wave hello this morning?" Clark asked his classmates over the table he and Oswald chose to sit at.

No one knew what he was talking about.

"You see?" Clark told his friend. "You made me take it down too soon."

"What did we miss?" asked one of the freshmen.

"You know the gentleman from Mills's introduction to the gastro-intestinal system?"

"The dead gentleman?"

"The same," Oswald confirmed. "Clark took it upon himself to decorate the foliage with his hand."

"I told you, that wasn't me," insisted Clark. "Well, not only me. At any rate, you had to see it for yourself. It's not funny in the telling."

"It wasn't funny in any event."

"Obviously I was playing to the wrong audience," Clark sulked.

It was at that moment that the first rock came smashing through one of the dining hall's windows. All talk and feasting came promptly to an end.

Eccleston University
April 11, 1846
2:11 pm

The siege was soon out of control. Angry shouts and protests turned to action and there was much destruction of property. What few students were outside sought refuge indoors, and those already inside didn't dare step out.

A rider was dispatched to summon the police. By the time the first officers arrived, no less than three outlying buildings on the campus were in flames and hundreds of windows in the main buildings broken. The doors had been barricaded from within out of desperation, but one was cleared to allow the officers entry so they could assess the situation.

Eighty-seven students were at that moment cornered on campus, along with another ten or so professors. The rest had fled the grounds at the earliest signs of violence. The mob had swelled to nearly double the number of the remaining student body and the police thought it prudent to remove them from the property entirely. The police presence had stemmed the acts of vandalism, but there was still the occasional stone flung from the fray and it was decided the situation could not be controlled so far from additional support. The students and their professors would have to be taken into protective custody.

With the police arranged in a phalanx formation, the retreating students and staff were escorted to town where they could be locked away behind more secure doors. The mob followed at a safe distance, their rage subdued for the moment, as they waited for a new target of their ire to present itself.

Tremane County Lockup
April 11, 1846
5:58 pm

Relocation to the county jailhouse had the detrimental effect of providing a more centralized location for rioters to assemble. Those who might not have been willing to commute all the way to the university campus now found themselves within a short walk of the hub of activity, and therefore able to join in the proceedings quite conveniently. The ranks grew accordingly.

Respect for the law and the integrity of the local lockup kept the mob at bay for the first hour. After that, stones and other refuse began to rain down on the bolted doors and barred windows of the jailhouse. Now that they were back in town, there was much more in the way of refuse to call upon as weapons and projectiles. The police swung their clubs at a few of the more aggressive attackers, but it was a futile show of force against so many who were still so angered. Forced back inside, they double locked the front gate and the steel door inside and hoped it would hold until the crowd exhausted itself.

"I wonder what has them so upset?" Clark wondered aloud, sitting in a cell next to Oswald. The cell door had been left open. No one was under arrest, but they felt like prisoners just the same.

"I can't make out a word they're saying," said Oswald. "It's all shouting and braying like animals. There's no sense to any of it."

Tremane County Lockup
April 11, 1846
10:09 pm

Once the mob had made up its collective mind to breech the gate and force its way into the jailhouse, there was no holding it back. One of the new telegraph poles, just installed late the previous year, was torn down and pressed into service as a battering ram. With the weight and strength of a dozen men behind it, the steel door buckled and folded in a matter of minutes.

The police did their valiant best to turn back the intruders, but there was only so much to be accomplished, club against brick, fist against broken bottle. They were overrun in moments, most of them rendered unconscious on the floor where they were additionally trampled by the vanguard of the mob as they made their way to the cells.

The students tried to protect themselves by swinging the cell doors shut and locking the masses out, but many of them had no time to manage even that. Few avoided being dragged into the street and beaten, and the best bet for most proved to be flight whenever they could successfully extract themselves from the grappling, the punching and the kicking.

The entire battle quickly descended into sheer chaos. Since so much rage was directed at so many unfamiliar faces, even the most bloodthirsty soon lost track of who was who in the swell of flailing bodies. In this way, some of the targets, mostly the older professors, were able to blend into the crowd and escape, while others in the mob fell upon their own kind, mistaking their neighbours and townsmen for the targeted offenders.

Thirteen students didn't survive the night. An additional four members of the mob were fatally injured, while one of the battered police officers lingered with a severe head injury to which he succumbed a full week later. There were eighteen dead in all.

Tremane County Lockup
April 12, 1846
12:04 am

Oswald Ainsworth was not one who lay among the dead. He instead found himself hanged, much like the instigating hand—not from an elm tree, but a lamppost on the street. After the street brawl that saw students fighting for their lives and rioters fighting for what they saw as justice, there was only enough energy left in the fracas to see one lone victim strung up in the name of vengeance for the defiled dearly departed. Oswald died without ever connecting the morning's prank to the evening's slaughter.

They cut him down in the morning, only once reinforcing police from another district confirmed the area was secure, and the other dead and injured had been removed from the scene.

Dilmore University
April 16, 1846
2:33 pm

Oswald, just like many of his fellow medical students, was a body donor. Through peer pressure and the implied promise of extra credit, about a third of all Eccleston students agreed, in principle, to repay their chosen profession with their own cadavers, so that they could further medical science in death as they sought to in life. Some took the extra step and entered into a legal contract with the university and its associates to donate their corpses to science when the time came. All assumed that such a time would not arrive for many years.

Oswald, being one of the rare dutiful examples who had made all the necessary arrangements already, soon found himself delivered, packed in ice, to another medical university in a whole other state three days after his unexpected demise. His original intention was for Eccleston to inherit his remains, but the administration considered it far too unsightly to ask their students to dissect the body of one of their own classmates. And so a trade with a sister institution was arranged. The students Oswald found himself lying under in the Dilmore University examination room were not at all dissimilar to himself and his roommate Clark, who had survived that night in the Tremane Lockup virtually unscathed.

Havers was a second year student, assisted by freshman Gilbert, who hadn't yet developed the stomach for this sort of thing. Havers was about to make his first incision into the chest cavity of the young man on the slab who would grow no older. He felt a twinge of pity for his novice assistant, who looked like he might be sick at the first sight of an organ or bone.

Havers caught Gilbert's eye and tried to lighten the mood.

"Want to see something funny?" he asked.

Hot Pennies

"YOU DON'T WANT to go to the hospital tonight, sweetie. The emergency room's full of crazies. I'll take you in the morning."

Kurt McGowan whimpered pathetically as he soaked his fingers in a bowl of ice water his mother had prepared for him. She was determined the burns weren't serious enough to race down to the hospital at this hour. Some cream and bandages and crushed children's Aspirin would hold her boy over for the night. But Kurt was just as determined to let the full extent of his pain be known to anyone within earshot. He wanted an audience of doctors and nurses to play to, just as he had two years earlier when he was eight and had broken his wrist during a particularly splendid bike crash.

A few more whimpers, maybe a soulful moan or two, and his doting mother would crack. She always did, she always would. She knew she was an easy touch, and was trying to take steps to harden her heart. The last thing she wanted was for her son to grow up with whining as his only means of manipulation. That would make him no better than his father.

Kurt's mother resolved to hold off for another hour. Or another half hour at least. Certainly she could wait and see if he settled down in the next fifteen minutes.

●　●　●

Anyone will tell you that New Year's Eve is the worst shift of all. Hands down, flat out, no doubt about it. The number of injuries is unparalleled, as is the amount of vomit that has the janitorial staff mopping the halls straight through till morning. There's one other annual occasion, however, that runs a close second. On a bad night, it can come very close to matching the injury and vomit quota. The one pivotal difference is the culprit behind it all. Alcohol is the root cause of New Year's mayhem, but it's sugar at the core of Hallowe'en.

November 1st was still several hours away and already the emergency room was brimming, filled to overflowing with the casualties of costume parties and trick-or-treatings and savage eggings. The kids started coming in as soon as the sun went down—the accidents, the injuries, the boo-boos filled the charts in record time. It would take all night to stitch everyone back together. By the time the sun was up again, the second wave of ailing children would begin to arrive. These would be the ones who had been up half the night gorging on goodies. They would be sick or simply nauseous, coming down hard from sugar highs, and desperate for something to settle their swollen bellies. One or two might need to have their stomachs pumped if they'd been especially gluttonous.

Neil Leverault hadn't volunteered for this. He'd worked at Templeton General long enough to know better, and was a physician with enough seniority to ditch the shit shifts. But this year he'd been outmanoeuvred. A particularly hot party hosted by a particularly hot nurse had drawn doctors from all levels of the medical hierarchy like flies. Most of them had been clever enough to arrange for time off weeks in advance. Others had merely called in sick at the last minute. This ultimately left Neil holding the bag along with a few other lonely souls who had little or no interest in popular parties or nurses who knew how to fill out a set of scrubs.

Neil inspected the rows of victims in the waiting room chairs. They were staggered in a wounded-child/concerned-parent-or-guardian pattern that repeated itself a couple of dozen times until there was standing room only. Templeton was small enough for Neil to know most of the kids by sight and most-frequent medical complaint.

Hugh Winburn was nine years old and suffered from chronic ear infections. Tonight he'd provoked a schoolmate who had dared tease him about his unimaginative clown costume. The schoolmate, dressed as an executioner complete with black mask and axe, had remained calm, even stoic, until Hugh suggested that his sister's Hallowe'en costume made her look even more like a whore than she usually did. That's when the executioner swung his halberd at him and landed a blow across Hugh's fingers. The halberd was only wood, painted silver to look like metal, and far too dull to cut anything. But it was still a solid ten pounds of lumber, and it handily crushed all four fingers that got in its way, breaking two.

Alan Jaycox was ten, and until tonight had never come to emergency with anything more serious than a bump or a scrape. Most of his hair had been scorched off an hour earlier when he thought it might be fun to toss a cherry bomb into a jack-o-lantern on his neighbour's porch. Unfortunately, the pumpkin had been lit by an oil lamp, and the whole thing went up with a deafening bang that sent flames and pulpy orange shrapnel flying up to thirty feet in all directions. Burns to Alan's scalp were only superficial. More serious burns were averted when an alert friend smothered Alan's blazing cape with his own more flame-retardant cloak.

Then there was Peter Paulson, eight and asthmatic, who had the dubious distinction of bringing an apocryphal urban legend to life by biting into an apple that really had a razor blade embedded in it. The blade had slipped neatly between his gapped front teeth and lodged itself deep into his gums as he bit down. He now sat next to his mother on one of the hard plastic waiting chairs, his mouth hanging open foolishly because he couldn't close it without causing further damage. It looked terribly painful, but the greatest injury was to Peter's pride. Unable to swallow effectively, he drooled a steady line of bloody saliva from his pulled-back lips. Peter was sure it made him look like an imbecile. He certainly felt like one for falling victim to that most legendary of Hallowe'en treat sabotages.

"How you doing, Pete?" asked Kurt McGowan as he entered the waiting room and spotted his third best friend slobbering all over himself. Kurt's mother was still at the registration desk, securing their place in line. Now that he was at the hospital, and away from the immediate presence of his mom, Kurt had shut off the waterworks and was dealing with the pain nicely.

"'ot 'oo 'ad e i 'on 'ite ow," answered Peter.

"You got it good," said Kurt, admiring Peter's wound. "Look what I got."

Kurt stuck his finger out, like he was pointing at Peter's nose. Peter leaned forward to inspect the damage. Most of Kurt's fingers on his right hand were red and blistering, but his index finger had been uniquely burned. Branded into the tip was an instantly recognizable profile of Her Majesty, Queen Elizabeth.

"'ool!" observed Peter, genuinely impressed.

● ● ●

"Trick or treat!" exclaimed the happy collection of boys and girls who had been making the rounds together for nearly an hour and were already weighed down with sacks of sweets.

Agnes Worthington had to hurry to get her treats out of the oven where they had been baking for the last twenty minutes at 360 degrees, just like her favourite brownie recipe. She threw her "kiss the cook" apron over her head and peeked inside with her thick bifocals, satisfying herself that her latest creation was quite done.

"Help yourselves, children," replied Mrs. Worthington, as she returned to the front door and held out the cookie tray in her oven-gloved hands.

The children dug in greedily. No one questioned why the cookie tray, fresh from the oven, held no cookies, chocolate chip or otherwise. Instead, the tray was brimming with a generous helping of pennies, shiny and new.

And piping hot.

Kurt McGowan, at the head of the group, was the first to start screaming once it was too late and his fingers were already buried up to the second knuckle. Most of the others were able to withdraw after an initial touch that sent a sharp searing signal of pain straight to their brains, warning of an ambush and not the generous UNICEF donation they had expected.

"Serves you right, you little bastards!" Mrs. Worthington screeched at the fleeing cowboys and astronauts, ballerinas and Raggedy Annes. "Little bastards!"

She wanted to curse out the horrid creatures some more, but Mrs. Worthington's lungs were old and her voice hoarse. She knew she couldn't project like she used to, back when she was a young mother and had first come to realize she secretly hated children—and not just the little coloured ones, either. Instead, Mrs. Worthington was forced to retire back into her home, to watch some more television and return the cookie tray of pennies to the oven in anticipation of the next group of candy beggars.

● ● ●

"At least it wasn't razor blades in the apples like Mr. Hayes on 12th."

This observation came from eleven-year-old Scotty Elmont who was, everyone agreed, the coolest kid at school. Kurt considered Scotty his number one best friend, but then so did a dozen other boys and one or two tomboys.

Scotty was neither sick nor injured, but was stuck in the emergency room just the same. His younger brother, Theo, was in anaphylactic shock after taking a bite of a peanut-laden candy bar. Their single dad had piled both boys in the car and rushed them over to the hospital within moments of Theo hitting the floor. Theo was now in a coma, which concerned no one. This sort of thing happened at least once, usually twice a year, and Theo had always fully recovered within a few days. Everyone was patiently waiting for the seven-year-old to get the picture and learn to leave the peanuts and the peanut butter and the peanut brittle well enough alone. But Theo, who was an otherwise bright young boy, seemed to have a blind spot when it came to his deadly allergy. At this point, Scotty was resigned to the idea that one day his brother would either learn or die. It was really up to him.

Peter nodded in agreement. His wound wasn't nearly as interesting as Kurt's, who could look forward to showing off his royal portrait for weeks until it began to heal over. Stitches—even stitches in his gums—wouldn't attract half the attention during recess and lunch.

"Someone ought to get Worthington back for that one," Scotty mused aloud as he picked at his stump. The spirit gum element of his favourite costume was starting to itch right at the juncture where his left arm used to be.

Scotty Elmont was never so happy to be an amputee as on Hallowe'en. He had made a custom of casting aside his prosthetic arm on that special occasion and painting his stump blood red so it would look like his missing limb had only recently been yanked off at the elbow. As he grew older, his makeup effects became more elaborate. Glue and stands of yarn did a fine job of simulating dangling ligaments and arteries, and when he was feeling extra ambitious, he'd affix an old ham bone to the tip of his truncated arm to simulate a humerus jutting out the end of a fresh wound. Once he felt he was sufficiently gory, he'd roam the streets trying to solicit handshakes from horrified passersby.

Without his artificial limb, Scotty was left with only one free hand to carry his candy, making it difficult to hold the bag open to receive more loot. But it was worth the inconvenience to have the most convincing maiming of any of the boys who revelled in walking around with fake axes buried in their heads, or ping-pong eyeballs popping out of their sockets. One year a young thalidomide victim had come to town, and Scotty was concerned he would have some stiff competition that Hallowe'en. The boy had no arms— just two flipper hands jutting out of his shoulders. Scotty saw the endless costume possibilities and was troubled. However, the thalidomide kid opted not to take advantage of his physical deformity, and made the trick-or-treating rounds in a disappointing hobo getup. Scotty reigned supreme for another year, but he was still glad when his only potential rival moved to another school district the following spring.

"Worthington and Hayes both," suggested Hugh Winburn as he came over to join the discussion.

"Nah. Hayes is harmless," concluded Alan Jaycox, who didn't want to be left out.

"You call tricking a kid into eating a razor harmless?" said Kurt, who felt obliged to speak for Peter since he could barely talk.

"He's nuts. Everyone knows to skip his house," Alan elaborated.

"Razor blades in apples are pretty mean, but you'd have to be a sucker to fall for that one," declared Scotty, who then added, "No offence, Pete."

"'un 'aken," replied Peter.

"Red-hot pennies, though. That's the product of a sick mind."

Everyone nodded silently, agreeing with Scotty's assessment.

"I think she's a witch," declared Kurt with such conviction, the other boys had to wonder if he was serious.

"What makes you think so?" asked Hugh.

"Because it's Hallowe'en, dummy."

And that reason seemed to satisfy everyone.

Scotty was the first to speak after several moments of contemplative silence.

"Well you know what they do to witches, don't you?"

● ● ●

Neil was just dismissing Todd Anderson, who tonight had graduated from chronic bed wetting to three stitches behind his left ear. The cause of the bed wetting was still a mystery, but the stitches were the results of a high-sticking incident with a trick-or-treater dressed as a favourite NHL goalie. Todd was supposed to be a vampire, but looked more like a spaceman. So many reflective safety strips covered his costume he could very nearly be seen from orbit. He insisted the hockey stick to the head had been a failed attempt to stake him for walking the earth as one of the undead. Neil suspected it had more to do with Todd's annoying habit of whistling when he breathed.

Neil was joined by a couple of residents who had just unloaded their own patients. According to the pecking order, Neil had first pick of any interesting cases on hand. Nothing really struck his fancy, but he found himself focusing on Peter. Peter was still wearing the rubber cowl from his costume since it couldn't be removed without jostling the protruding razor blade. Neil decided it provided an interesting complication to a procedure that might not otherwise keep him awake for the next ten minutes.

"I'll take Batman," he announced, and left the two residents to fight over his leftovers.

Peter's mother came to lead her son away from his roundtable meeting with the other neighbourhood boys. He was reluctant to leave his friends, and even more reluctant to face the razor extraction, but the original focus of the discussion had already come to its conclusion. The beginnings of a plot had been formed, and now the topic of conversation had switched to more pressing points of debate like comic books and sports cards.

● ● ●

Traditionally speaking, if you knock on a door and don't get a treat, you're supposed to deliver your trick in a reasonable amount of time. On or near Hallowe'en is accepted protocol. The boys didn't understand that there was a statute of limitations on Hallowe'en tricks, so their revenge was plotted for Christmas. The intervening weeks were used to heal their wounds and come up with something audacious. It was Scotty, having survived the night unscathed, who did most of the legwork in preparation for D-day. This involved nearly nightly trips to Mrs. Worthington's house under cover of darkness with a file and a can of lighter fluid.

The police had stopped by once to respond to complaints about Agnes Worthington's nasty Hallowe'en prank that had hurt a couple dozen children—none too seriously. They ultimately decided not to press charges, even after she accused the officers of being agents of Satan and threatened to turn the garden hose on them. Mrs. Worthington was the sort of neighbour who inspired plenty of complaints, but none so serious as to require a court appearance. City prosecutors wanted no part of seeking fines or jail time for the petty crimes of a woman who looked like everyone's favourite aunt or grandmother, especially when any accusations could be countered with claims of senility or mental illness. They once tried to pin a series of cat poisonings on her, but abandoned that idea due to lack of evidence. The oven-roasted pennies incident had been her most serious infraction since the last of six cats had vomited and died within a hundred yards of her house years earlier. Perhaps things might have turned out better for all involved if the justice system had pursued retribution this time around, but once again the police and prosecutors decided to leave well enough alone.

One of the most common complaints about Mrs. Worthington was her vintage Christmas lights. They were vintage through age rather than design, having been up for almost thirty consecutive years. Stringing them around the front windows of the house and over the porch's eaves trough was the last service her husband had performed for her before he finally packed up their children and left her for a woman half her age and twice as hateful. Her neighbours were fed up with looking at them year round, and few could deny that a string of Christmas lights stopped being festive by March. A proposed city ordinance addressing the tardy removal of Christmas decorations was bogged down in bureaucracy, but remained alive due, in part, to the three-decade-and-counting run of the Worthington lights.

It was the Christmas lights that drew Scotty's attention during his nightly trespasses. The whole neighbourhood knew from experience that Mrs. Worthington plugged in her Christmas lights exactly once a year for about twenty-four hours, from Christmas Eve to Christmas night. Then they went off again for another year. Scotty saw a window of opportunity for vengeance and was determined to seize it.

The rest of the boys, for their part, limited themselves to acting as Scotty's personal cheering section, urging him on, assuring him that this was a brilliant idea that would go off without a hitch, but closely guarding their plausible deniability should things go badly. Sneaking onto Mrs. Worthington's porch each night, Scotty would cup one of the colourful Christmas bulbs in the blunt double-pronged hook of his prosthetic arm and then patiently saw away at a small section of the glass with the iron file he had liberated from under his father's work bench. Once he had ground enough of the thin glass shell away to make a small hole, he would poke the nozzle of his can of lighter fluid into the bulb and fill it until the liquid touched the tip of the filament inside. He would then repeat this procedure on the next Christmas light in line. It was highly delicate work, but years of model-aircraft construction had given Scotty a light touch, and he broke only two bulbs outright, and slightly cracked another three.

Each night, Scotty would try to work through at least six bulbs, averaging ten, and managing as many as twenty on one particularly productive evening. By the time the sun had risen on the morning of Christmas Eve, Scotty had successfully sabotaged over four hundred individual lights all across Mrs. Worthington's front porch, from the eves, down the support posts, and woven through the slatted wooden rails on the deck. He never managed to get to all of them, but he figured his ambitious project had accounted for over seventy-five percent of the entire daisy-chain.

Getting out of the house after dark on Christmas Eve was a simple matter for all the boys in on the scheme. They had planted the seed of an excuse weeks earlier, claiming an organized carolling excursion which, all the parents agreed, sounded absolutely adorable. Many of the parents wanted to come along and take pictures for the family album, but each of the boys was armed with the same plea for their moms and dads to please not embarrass them in front of their school buddies. They promised there would be ample photo ops when the group eventually came around to their own house to offer something fairly traditional and reasonably on-key. Of course, there was no intention to ever utter a single seasonal note. If the carollers were questioned about being no-shows, the agreed-upon story was that they had all gotten cold after working the first couple of blocks and accepted one neighbour's invitation inside for a round of hot chocolate. Time, they would claim, just slipped away after that.

The first few kids gathered outside the Worthington house late in the afternoon, a good hour before sunset. Nobody wanted to miss the fireworks, and there was no set time for the lights to turn on. Sometime after dark was the closest anyone could estimate. Word had spread throughout the entire school about the impending spectacle, and by the time the crisp winter sky lit up red with a breathtaking sunset no one had the slightest interest in looking at, the street in front of Mrs. Worthington's bungalow was packed with a playground's-worth of children.

About half an hour after the sun dipped under the horizon of rooftops and the streetlights all came on, the main event started without any fanfare or warning. Somewhere in the house, a plug had been pushed into an electrical socket, sparking hundreds of light bulb filaments right over hundreds of tiny reservoirs of lighter fluid. It happened with such a complete lack of warning, only a handful of the audience happened to be looking directly at the Worthington house at the moment of ignition. What they saw was the string of lights exploding in a line of white flashes that dripped blazing dollops of lighter fluid into the hedges. Glass shrapnel from the bulbs made it as far as the curb, but none of the observers was hit.

After an initial group-gasp reaction from the crowd, there was a smattering of laughter and a few isolated pockets of applause. The commotion died down quickly, and the first couple of minutes following the initial bang were anticlimactic. The flames licked at the house's aluminium siding and brick walls, failing to get a foothold. The porch was a wood structure, however, and the edges of the roof flickered with a low flame that struggled for survival against the damp wood. Just when it looked like the disappointing blaze would burn out all by itself, large plumes of smoke started to rise from between the shingles. The flames had managed to worm their way under the roof and find plenty of dry timber in the rafters of the attic crawlspace. As the entire roof started to catch, it seemed this would be a reasonably spectacular inferno after all. The audience looked on quietly, content in the assumption that one of the neighbours would notice and call the fire department.

The emergency-room conspirators watched the fire spread, unsure if this had been the ultimate plan all along, afraid to say anything just in case they were the only one in the group who had thought this was supposed to begin and end with the destruction of some universally loathed Christmas lights. From a safe distance, they examined the Worthington house for any sign of life or movement.

"Jeezuz," said Alan, who had been warned repeatedly against using the Lord's name in vain around the holidays and avoided this sin through mispronunciation, "That's Scotty in there!"

Sure enough, standing in the centre of the living room window, poking through Mrs. Worthington's drab off-white curtains, was Scotty, waving both his stump and his one good arm at them frantically. He wasn't wearing his prosthetic limb, but where he may have misplaced it seemed to be the least of Scotty's worries at the moment. There was mortal panic written all over his face.

● ● ●

Scotty had woken up early on December 24th after a
poor night's sleep. Something was nagging at him, but
he was at a loss to pinpoint exactly what. He ate little
at breakfast with his brother, and was so distracted he
almost neglected to discourage Theo from spreading
peanut butter on his toast. It was nearly lunch by the
time Scotty pinpointed the source of his nagging
concern—what he had done to the Worthington
house. It wasn't that his petty act of vandalism might
ultimately escalate into full-scale arson, but rather that
his weeks of effort might all come to naught. He
remembered the last time he had employed his father's
favourite brand-name lighter fluid, when he used half a
can to burn out a prodigious ant hill. The leftovers had
evaporated by the time some stubborn charcoal
briquettes needed to be helped along. Barbeques were
uncommon at the Elmont homestead, and months
had passed before Scotty's father discovered his son
had left the cap off. Now Scotty found himself
wondering how many of his sabotaged Christmas
bulbs may have gone dry since he first began his
project.

That afternoon, Scotty decided to swing by the
Worthington house with his can of lighter fluid to
make sure the evening's show would be every bit as
spectacular as he'd originally envisioned. Although
there remained enough lighter fluid collected at the
bottom of each bulb to assure near-total destruction of
the entire string of lights, some of the earliest filed and
filled bulbs were running low. Scotty had never

intruded on the Worthington property by the light of day, but he decided to risk it this one time in order to top off a dozen or so bulbs he thought needed a full tank of fuel to explode with maximum effect.

Scotty never heard Mrs. Worthington approach. He felt her first—specifically her gnarled fingernails, thick with many layers of nail polish, digging into his flesh as she grabbed him by the rim of his ear and pulled him inside her house. There was nobody on the street to catch Scotty's cry of protest, and once the door slammed shut behind him, any chance of someone hearing was extinguished.

Mrs. Worthington turned the latch on the door and proceeded to drag Scotty down the hall and into her kitchen. He didn't dare struggle for fear of splitting his ear open on her claws.

"I don't care for children snooping around my property. I don't care for children at all, but children on my property get under my skin. I'd sic the dogs on you if I kept any of the filthy beasts. What are you doing here and don't give me lies!"

Mrs. Worthington released Scotty and stared him down, waiting for an answer. Scotty couldn't think of any reasonable explanation for his presence, so he simply said the first thing that came to mind. As it happened, it was closer to the truth than he'd ever intended to get, not that Mrs. Worthington recognized or appreciated it.

"Trick or treat?"

Mrs. Worthington looked Scotty up and down for a long time.

"Boy, are you stupid in the head?" she said.

Scotty wasn't sure what to say. He certainly felt stupid for being nabbed so easily.

"Seems brains aren't all you're missing. How'd you lose that?" asked Mrs. Worthington, pointing her chin at Scotty's artificial limb. "Horsing around where you shouldn't have, I'd say."

"I guess so," Scotty agreed, glad to avoid recounting a more detailed history.

Mrs. Worthington grabbed Scotty by the shoulders and spun him around so his back was facing her. Pulling down the collar of his coat, exposing some bare neck, she reached for a large pair of scissors that hung from a hook that was hammered into the faded pot-and-kettle wallpaper of her kitchen. Scotty felt the cold metal of the scissor blades slide across the back of his shirt before slipping under one of the leather straps that held his prosthetic arm in place. One forceful snip later and Mrs. Worthington was through the strap. The limb came free and dangled loosely. With a sharp tug on the hook end of Scotty's arm, Mrs. Worthington yanked it out of the sleeve of his coat.

"Hey! Give it back!" Scotty protested.

Mrs. Worthington tossed the limb onto the top of her refrigerator with a careless backhanded fling. It landed at the rear of the greasy appliance surface, well out of reach of the boy who was still a few years away from achieving his full height.

"You'll get it back when I'm satisfied with the job you've done."

"What job?" Scotty asked, not even trying to mask his suspicious dread.

"The job that makes amends for your snooping around and horsing around and whatnot."

● ● ●

"Scotty!" Kurt yelled through the thick oak wood, "Unlock the door!"

Of his stunned and amazed friends, Kurt was the only one who ran to the Worthington house to help.

"I can't!" Scotty yelled back.

Unlocking the door from the inside meant turning a latch and the door knob at the same time. Two hands were required to accomplish this and, despite his best efforts, Scotty soon discovered that one hand and a stump simply weren't up to the task. After two solid hours of toil, he still hadn't earned his arm back. Not to Mrs. Worthington's satisfaction.

The job Scotty had been unwillingly recruited for would haunt him for the rest of his days. Pulling Mrs. Worthington's oven out from the wall had merely been backbreaking. Scrubbing the floor underneath it was both backbreaking and horrifying. The linoleum was coated in decades of spillage and dust that had turned black as it developed the consistency of tar. Scotty had to fight his gag reflex as he scraped at it with soapy water and a stiff brush, especially when he spotted something that he could actually identify as food. A single dry noodle or fossilized pea was somehow even more sickening than the sea of filth they came to be stuck in. A routine of scrubbing and soaking, scrubbing and soaking set in and Scotty lost all track of time. He didn't even realize night had fallen when Mrs. Worthington grunted and raised herself out of her ratty recliner one final time, tearing herself away from her television stories. He thought she was coming to check on his progress and criticize his work ethic again, but she turned left instead of right when she hit the hall. He couldn't imagine what she was up to until he heard her wheezing as she bent down to push a plug into a spare socket. Scotty wasted a critical moment deciding whether he should shout "Wait!" "Stop!" or "Don't!"—not that a single word of warning would have done a thing to discourage Mrs. Worthington from turning on her Christmas lights.

"What about the back door?" Kurt suggested.

"I already tried! It's no good!" The back door lock had been an even more complex mix of latches and knobs. Scotty was unsure how Mrs. Worthington ever got it open without three hands.

"Can you open a window?"

"I'll try."

Scotty retreated back into the burning building that was starting to fill with smoke. All the windows he'd seen so far had been painted shut. He figured it was about time to find something he could use to break one. It had to be hefty enough to smash the glass and knock out all the shards around the edges, but light enough that Scotty could pick it up and swing it with one hand. Nothing in the immediate vicinity fit the bill and the thickening smoke was reducing visibility quickly, making it harder to find something suitable with every passing moment.

Scotty could hear Mrs. Worthington hacking somewhere in the house, lost in dense fumes. She roared with a smoker's cough that was earned years before her house started burning all around her. Even as the roof began to cave in with a tremendous crash of splitting beams, Mrs. Worthington's fearsome cough was the loudest noise Scotty could hear. It sounded like an evil chortle, punctuated by a distinct chanting whisper, "Little bastard, little bastard, where have you got to?"

Scotty was certain if she got her claws into him again, she wouldn't let go. Mrs. Worthington would hold on tight until the whole house burned to the ground and all they would ever find of him would be the metal hook of his lost arm.

Outside, Kurt was determined to keep up his end of the rescue. He ran through the crunching remains of hundreds of burst Christmas lights, looking for an alternate exit for Scotty. His eyes fell on a basement window, poking up above the snow line. Kurt pressed his face to the glass and cupped his hands around his eyes, peering inside. The latch was open, but he could see nothing but black beyond the window frame. It took nearly a full minute of pushing at the top and scratching at the base to pry the window open—plenty of time for the fire to spread from the attic to the ground floor.

Kurt poked his head through the window and looked around as his eyes adjusted to the dark. The basement was nothing but open walls and storage space. Boxes were piled high, all the way up to the open window, and Kurt figured they could be scaled easily provided they were full of non-breakables. He swung a leg inside and put some weight on the top box, testing it to make sure it offered a solid foothold. It did, right up until Kurt slipped and fell. The entire pile of boxes held strong, making his tumble into the basement that much more bruise-inducing. He landed face-down on the concrete floor and felt the cool stone on his cheek. It took him a moment to regain his senses and remember there was a very hot inferno consuming everything in its path just one floor above.

Kurt picked himself up and started shouting, "Scotty! Get to the basement! I found a way out!"

Kurt could hear Scotty's heavy footfalls above his head as his friend searched for the door to the basement. Kurt looked around, too scared to venture farther inside, not quite ready to retreat back out the window. This was the lair local kids speculated about, often wildly, never accurately. Disappointingly, it looked like any other unfinished basement Kurt had seen in his life, with a bare floor and walls made mostly of wooden cross beams and supports. The only difference was the amount of clutter—unhappy decades' worth, piled on memories best forgotten. Kurt was calculating the age of some of the furniture based on the coats of dust when he spotted...*it*.

There, sitting on one cross beam, deep in the recess of an exposed wall, was a pickle jar filled to the rim with a fortune in pennies. Long since cooled after the end of the Hallowe'en festivities, they waited patiently for their next trip to the oven and the inevitable visit from greedy trick-or-treaters. Or at least for the next time Mrs. Worthington bothered to roll them and bring them to the bank.

"Treasure," Kurt said aloud under his breath. "Witch treasure."

Distracted by the allure of the Hallowe'en bounty he'd been denied nearly two months earlier, Kurt found himself reaching into the secret hiding place he'd discovered. It would only take a moment to snatch his prize, and then Kurt would be able to spend the holidays rattling his penny jar at his friends and bragging about the treasure he'd captured from the very bowels of the witch's den. He was pretty sure pennies didn't count as real theft and wouldn't result in criminal charges, or worse, a grounding.

Digging deep, his arm buried into the recess of the wall up to his shoulder, Kurt was just able to touch the penny jar with the tips of his fingers. He stretched, trying to hook the jar lid with his fingernails. Instead of finding the grip he was looking for, Kurt only managed to push the jar off the far edge of the wooden beam it was perched on. The penny jar plummeted to the concrete floor and shattered, sending its fortune scattering in all directions. What he thought had been a secret hiding place had actually been an obscured view of the open space on the other side.

Kurt started to withdraw his arm until he felt a terrible stabbing pain in his forearm. The pain was so sharp and unexpected, it took a moment for him to realize it was actually several terrible stabbing pains all at once. He winced, but held his screams to himself. With that old witch Worthington upstairs somewhere, Scotty in need of rescue, and the whole house in flames, now didn't seem like the time to add to the chaos with a bunch of panicked yelling and hollering, even when his arm hurt more than anything ever.

Kurt ducked his head down to look into the hole in the wall and see what it was that had grabbed onto his arm like a mouthful of shark teeth. Jutting from various cross beams inside, Kurt could see a number of nails sticking out. They had all been hastily bent and hammered down by the construction workers who had built the house a million years ago. Angled away from where Kurt stood, he had been able to worm his arm past them unharmed. But now that he was trying to pull back out, the nail tips were hooked under his skin in several spots. A few of them looked deep, all looked rusty.

That was bound to earn a tetanus booster shot, thought Kurt.

He tried to pull his arm free, but that only made the rusty nails dig further under his skin. The pain shot all the way up his arm and into his head, bouncing around inside his skull like ricocheting bullets. He was sure if he pulled any harder, the nails would peel the flesh off his whole arm like an elbow-length glove.

"What are you standing around for? We gotta go!"

Scotty had finally found the route to the basement and was now standing impatiently at Kurt's side, tugging at his coat with his one hand, prodding him towards the open window with his stump.

"I'm stuck!" Kurt protested against Scotty's persistent jostling.

"How stuck?"

Scotty didn't wait for the details. He ducked his head and had a look down the hole where he could see the many nails chewing into Kurt's arm for himself.

"That is super-fucking stuck," Scotty concluded. "Wait here! I'll find something to get you out."

For as long as he dared, Scotty searched the basement for a tool that would help him set Kurt free. The fire upstairs was spreading quickly and licks of flame were probing through the floorboards above their heads, dropping embers into the cellar, looking for new fuel to ignite. There was plenty waiting, all of it dry and highly flammable. When Scotty finally returned to Kurt's side, he brought only one tool with him—apparently the only tool the decidedly unhandy Agnes Worthington had ever owned. It was a hatchet and it was far down Scotty's mental list of items he would have preferred to use to get the job done.

Kurt looked at the hatchet in Scotty's one good hand. It was old and spotted with corrosion, but still sharp. Kurt nodded in resignation. He could see the fear in Scotty's eyes. It told him there was no other option, and if there had been, Scotty would have seized it in an instant rather than go through with this particular plan.

Kurt closed his eyes, bracing for a pain he knew would be far worse than what he was already imagining. "Just try to get it off in one good shot."

● ● ●

It took three.

What happened after that was a blur to Scotty, who felt woozy from what he had just watched himself do, and a total blackout of memory to Kurt. With his one hand hooked under Kurt's armpit, Scotty managed to half-drag and half-carry him up the hill of old boxes and antique furniture until he was able to shove Kurt back out through the basement window.

When their friends saw the two boys scrambling out of the blazing house, a few of the braver ones ran forward to help them get clear of the building. Scotty collapsed to the ground, coughing uncontrollably, while some of the other boys slapped his back unhelpfully. Everyone was still reacting to the amount of Kurt's blood they'd managed to get all over themselves when they noticed that Kurt himself was nowhere to be seen.

"Where'd he go?" one wondered aloud.

It didn't take a great tracker to figure it out. The blood trail in the snow was obvious, leading away across Mrs. Worthington's property and into the street.

Kurt lived only a couple of blocks away. Even out of his head with pain and shock and blood loss, he was able to find his way home on autopilot, gripping his open wound tightly with his remaining hand, slowing the flow of blood just enough to keep himself alive. Kurt only let go of his pumping artery to let himself in through the front door. He stumbled through the house, tracking snow and mud and blood across his mother's nice clean floors, until he found her in the living room laying presents under the Christmas tree.

"I don't think we should wait to go to the hospital this time," he announced before collapsing.

• • •

The third worst shift of all was Christmas. Nobody wanted to be stuck servicing seasonal injuries during a holiday that was reserved for giving and receiving and reconnecting with family and friends. Even the Jews on the staff didn't want to get stuck with the Christmas shift, and usually spent most of December trying to negotiate for the time off. Christmas injuries and illnesses weren't as plentiful or specific as on other occasions. Mostly they amounted to the usual sort of patient complaints that come in wintertime, such as falls and collisions due to icy conditions. Come Christmas morning, however, you could always count on one or two incidents arising from novices trying out their expensive new Christmas gifts. Power tools usually.

It hadn't been a power tool that had lobbed off one boy's arm at the elbow. It had been something more primitive, like an axe. Maybe the result of a firewood chopping accident. Neil didn't ask. The mother seemed completely clueless and all the boy would say was how disappointed he was that he had to lose the one with his unique Queen Elizabeth brand. It was the painkillers talking. The police could fish for more details if they were interested. For his part, Neil was done with the triage and was satisfied the kid was stable enough to be sent upstairs for more stitches and a transfusion. Right now he was stuck dealing with some crazy old lady with smoke inhalation on top of a four-pack-a-day cough. She'd been found wandering the streets without proper winter attire and making little to no sense. What clothes she wore were blackened and burned in places, but otherwise she seemed to have survived her ordeal—whatever it may have been—perfectly intact. It was a Christmas miracle. Physically she seemed fine.

"Go straight to hell you bastard," the old lady told Neil when he first approached her to make his basic assessment.

Mentally it was another matter. The old lady hacked violently and spat some sooty phlegm in Neil's face. She cackled, amused at her own proficient aim. Social services would be called and she would quickly and efficiently be filed away into the system. The sooner the better. Neil still felt bad about some of the hard-luck cases that passed through his emergency room. Others he couldn't wait to be rid of, Christmas miracle or not.

"Hey, Neil. Congrats on the trifecta," one senior resident called out in passing.

"What are you talking about?"

"They just posted the schedule for next week. Guess who pulled the New Year's Eve shift."

● ● ●

Scotty never went trick or treating as the one-armed boy again. Somehow it didn't seem as amusing as it once did. Come the next Hallowe'en, he teamed up with Kurt and they went out as the two-headed monster. Kurt supplied the left arm, Scotty the right. Both boys performed one head each.

Of his dozen potential best friends, Scotty had finally settled on one.

Table d'hôte

I DON'T LIKE being the middleman, but if there are favours owed and money on the table, I'll make the appropriate introductions, arrange a meeting between talent and client, make sure everybody is playing nice. Then I get the hell out of the way and let the deal happen or not.

Robbie needed a job done. Wanted more than needed, really. But he was calling in a favour, he had the money to make it happen, and who am I to judge? He wanted a man dead and I knew people who could handle the job. I cared about Robbie. He was a nice enough guy when he didn't have murder on his mind. This was uncharted territory for him, so I wanted to make sure he didn't go slumming. Left to his own devices, he probably would have hired some junkie scumbag who'd turn him in the next time he got pinched on a possession charge. No, this had to be done right, by a professional, or Robbie would end up screwing himself.

We met at a restaurant, the three of us. Robbie, myself and the European. I didn't know the European's name or country of origin, but the mannered way he spoke made me think of Europe. We sat together in a booth in the back, over drinks and a bowl of mixed nuts. I chose an unpopular restaurant with bad reviews and was rewarded with no other customers and terrible service. We were left alone, with no one nearby who might listen in.

I had briefed the European about Robbie's needs and the fact that this was all new to him. He agreed to help hold Robbie's hand as we walked him through the process.

"I'm a practical man. I understand practical things," the European told Robbie. "There are many practical reasons to want somebody dead. Economic reasons usually. Political sometimes. Other motivations arise. There's jealousy and revenge—very common. These are impractical reasons for murder, but there's nothing that says such a killing can't be handled in a practical way. This is my method."

A word of caution crept into his voice as he picked at the bowl of nuts.

"Sometimes the client wants something extra. They want me to pull out fingernails, cut balls off, make the mark beg for death. I always refuse these jobs. There are sick bastards out there who will do these things for less money and the pleasure such sadism gives them. I want no part of it. If you want someone—anyone—dead, I can make that happen quickly, cleanly, efficiently. But do not expect extras. The menu I offer may be limited, too specialized for some. But my product is of the highest quality. And there are always paying customers who appreciate a quality product."

He cracked a stubborn walnut and scattered the fragments across the table cloth, picking through the bits of shell for crumbs of meat.

"Murder?" he added, "This I can do. Cruelty?"

He wagged a disapproving finger, "This I will not do."

"So what then, you kill them with kindness?"

Sitting on the padded bench in the booth next to Robbie, I elbowed him in the ribs. This was not a man to offend, and he didn't like clients getting cute.

"No, I kill them with bullets. Don't be such a fucking smartass," said the European.

"Please excuse my friend. This is his first time," I apologized.

"As you've mentioned," replied the European. He turned back to Robbie.

"So who is this person you wish dead?"

There was a lengthy silence across the table as Robbie and the European stared at each other. It was only ended by a single gunshot I never saw coming.

"His eyes," the European told me, "pointed at you."

Robbie tipped forward in his seat and slammed face-first into the table. I could clearly see the empty cavity where his brains once were through the exit wound in the back of his skull. The European slipped his handgun back into his coat pocket and stood.

We left abruptly without paying the bill. In this business, money counts for much, friendship counts for little, but professional courtesy is everything.

One Last Time

MRS. BLACK WAS QUITE MAD by the time they found her, eight days after her husband had died in the throes of passion.

On a Saturday night, after a dozen beers at the bar on fifth street, Mr. Black, a three-hundred-and-fourteen-pound construction worker, returned home to his waiting wife of eighteen years. She was a frail woman, approaching fifty years and ninety pounds. They were an odd match—Mrs. Black a small introverted book-reader, Mr. Black a large gregarious fellow. They did, however, love each other enough to stick together for nearly two decades, despite regular financial problems and occasional arguments generated by Mrs. Black's reticence and Mr. Black's weekend drinking binges.

On this particular Saturday night, as with most others, when Mr. Black came home inebriated, scratching at the front door with his key as he searched for the lock, Mrs. Black sat in the living room reading a romance novel. She listened for a full minute until her husband found the keyhole and let himself in. Greeting him from her seat, she watched as he walked unsteadily into the kitchen to find a bag of potato chips to eat. By the time he came back, Mrs. Black had carefully placed a tasselled bookmark between pages 124 and 125, and laid her book down on a table next to the couch. She sat, her hands folded in her lap, looking straight-faced up at her husband, waiting for the grin she knew was coming.

When Mr. Black did finally grin, it was an honest, albeit lecherous one, directed at his wife between potato chip-salted lips. At this signal, she stood, fastidiously straightened her skirt, and walked ahead of him up the stairs. He followed, leaning on the steps with one hand as he turned the initial corner at the base of the staircase. With his free hand, he reached out and pinched his wife's behind slightly more roughly than he might have had he been sober. Mr. Black rarely touched his wife when sober though, and certainly never sexually. For the last several years of their life together, Mr. and Mrs. Black had only engaged in sexual intercourse on Saturday nights, after Mr. Black had gotten at least five beers into himself. They would skip the occasional week, but generally he was punctual.

Once in their bedroom, Mrs. Black stripped quietly, passionlessly, somewhat bored. She didn't resent her weekly chores under the covers because she loved her husband. Somewhere along the way though, sex had lost any mystique or excitement it ever held for her. Such sexual thrills lived on for her only in the pulp novels she read which were, she acknowledged, a fantasy far removed from her own life.

She lay naked under the single sheet of the bed. By this time her husband had managed to undo his belt buckle and drop his pants to his ankles. Leaving his stained t-shirt on, he mounted his wife, penetrated her, and buried his face in her shoulder, groaning. Mrs. Black was dry, but her husband pumped at her anyway, like a slow laborious machine. She stared silently at the ceiling and thought, as she had last Saturday and the Saturday before that, that she should get Mr. Black to paint over the cracks up there before the summer ended. She tried not to think about her husband, rolling his fat belly over her body rhythmically, fantasizing about the centrefolds of his youth so he could keep enough of an erection for the time he needed to come.

Two minutes later Mr. Black groaned slightly louder than he had upon penetration, convulsed briefly, and went limp atop his wife. Several minutes passed before Mrs. Black called quietly to her husband to please roll over and sleep on his side of the bed. She repeated her request more loudly a moment later, but there was still no response. She tried to roll him over herself, but was overwhelmingly outweighed and pinned under him in such an awkward way as to allow her no movement. She had left her right arm above the sheet and now used her free hand to tap him on the back insistently, jabbing him lightly with her fingernail.

Mr. Black did not wake up.

Mrs. Black began to consider her husband now, inside of her. She could still feel his erection, unmoving but solid. He had not remained hard after orgasm since their wedding night, and Mrs. Black wondered if he was going to make love to her again like he had on that one occasion and not since. But his stillness was disturbing. She realized for the first time that she could no longer feel his heavy breathing on her neck where his head was still pressed. She could not feel his excited heartbeat calming down after his exertion, thumping under his shirt. She felt no signs of life in her husband at all, and understood that the weight-induced heart attack the doctor had warned him about had finally claimed him at the age of fifty-three.

In a sudden panic, Mrs. Black thrashed violently under her husband's bulk, trying to free herself. There was no space to permit much motion, and after only a few seconds of struggling Mrs. Black stopped, panting. The mass of her husband pushed down on her heavily, and for one moment Mrs. Black thought she would not be able to catch her breath. She tried to escape from under her husband twice more, each time getting more exhausted and breathless. Three hundred pounds continued to pin her in place—an unmoveable burden for her small and weak frame. She was stuck in this position, like an animal clamped in a trap.

She tried to scream—scream for anyone outside who might possibly hear and come to pull her husband's dead body off of her. She could only try. With the weight on her chest, she could barely breathe enough to keep from passing out, let alone to inhale deeply and cry out. So Mrs. Black lay there under the rolls of dead flesh that used to be her husband, and cried softly in fear and grief until she fell asleep.

It was a hot August morning when she woke up again, gasping. Her body had strained for air all night as she slept, forcing her to half-wake several times just to get a better lung's worth. Now she was fully awake and breathing laboriously, having to make a conscious effort to acquire each drag of oxygen. Mr. Black had gone stiff during the night. She could feel his hardened muscles each time she achieved a slight shift in position. His stomach and chest had turned purple as blood came to rest at the lowest points in his body. His penis had lost its erection, but remained flaccid inside her. She wiggled her hips as much as she could manage, but it refused to drop out. She gave up as soon as she felt strained, not wanting to put herself through another long period of breathlessness again.

Mrs. Black lay quietly for several hours as the morning passed into early afternoon. Occasionally, she would hear people outside and try to make enough noise for them to notice. Always, she would stop abruptly after a few moments, wheezing for air. There were not many occasions for her to attempt to make noise anyway. That end of town by the train tracks was sparsely populated. Freight trains rumbled by more frequently than neighbours.

It was nearly one o'clock when Mrs. Black decided there was no avoiding it, loosened up, and urinated. She had not peed her bed since she was eight, but circumstances deemed it necessary. She had tried to occupy herself with concentrating on her hunger, but that offered little distraction. She had needed to go all morning, and since no one was hurrying to help her, she decided to avoid further discomfort. The warm liquid trickled easily from her despite the dead flesh pressed against her groin. Her thighs were dampened as it pooled under her pelvis and soaked into the mattress. It took only a few moments for Mrs. Black to adjust to the wet sensation. Her relief outweighed any new discomfort.

There was a clock on a shelf by the end of the bed but Mrs. Black could not lean forward enough to see it. Instead, she relied on the sun shining through the window to her right for reference. It faced west, and she watched as the light shone in more brightly as time passed. She judged that it was perhaps three o'clock when the flies came.

The rip in the window screen had been there since last fall. Mr. Black hadn't bothered to repair it then, or during the whole current summer. It had grown larger and larger as, every few days, Mrs. Black poked her fingers through it and idly wondered when it would be fixed or replaced. There had been no immediate need for a new screen. The early summer months had been uncommonly cold, and the Blacks were only visited by an occasionally mosquito or two. Mrs. Black had recently begun to nag her husband about it again when August came and the weather warmed enough for one good heat wave before the start of fall. The house had had more insects in it these past few weeks, and the screen had been ripped going on a year now. Mrs. Black thought her husband had mentioned buying some new mesh screening just a day or so ago. She couldn't quite remember. Regardless, it was still torn now, and the flies had easy access to the bedroom.

Mrs. Black noticed no foul smell coming from her dead husband's corpse, but then bugs are more sensitive to these things she supposed. The stink of the urine-soaked sheets on top of it had probably helped draw them in for a look. She watched as a few buzzed above Mr. Black's back in tight circles, landing every few seconds to test the grounds, and then taking off to search for a better patch. Mrs. Black observed them intently, having had nothing interesting to do for the hours before their arrival. She saw how they would walk around on her husband in quick darting motions, stop a moment, and continue on their way a second later. If she moved her head slightly, they would take off for a minute, until they were sure there was no danger, and then return. Mrs. Black had seen many flies before—swooping down on picnic sandwiches and sweaty horses. She had never actually examined them, though. But now, stuck in her unfortunate vantage point, she let herself be fascinated by them. She counted four different ones that afternoon. They stayed several hours, and finally left as the evening approached and the sun sank—perhaps retreating to the corners of the room, or maybe leaving again through the hole in the screen window.

The day had been hot, upward in the nineties. Mrs. Black had not been too bothered by it, despite her position. Her husband had cooled to a cozy room temperature, and Mrs. Black was naked with only a thin sheet covering her and her husband's lower halves. The temperature dropped slightly for the night, and Mrs. Black was able to sleep better than she had the previous evening.

Mrs. Black needed a drink when she awoke. She instinctively tried to get up at first, but remembered her predicament and lay back to think. She had been able to ignore the hunger that plagued her all during the day before and still did, but it was the thirst now that stuck in her mind, unavoidable. Water was entirely unobtainable, and so Mrs. Black resolved that the only solution was to drink her own urine. She had read that sailors trapped aboard lifeboats for weeks survived that way. The thought had disgusted her then, but was now welcome as the only means to lubricate her scaly throat.

When she tried to place her cupped hand to catch some liquid however, she found that her husband's heavy leg blocked the way. His muscles had loosened up again during the night, but he was still immoveable, and she was unable to work her hand into position. She tried to reach in between the back of his two legs, but they were lying together, too thick to spread. It was only two hours later, when the thirst was far beyond ignoring and had become the central focus of every moment's thought, that she accepted what she must do.

Mr. Black's belly was bruised and swollen with the blood that had come to settle there. The roll of fat that hung over Mrs. Black's side was thick and inviting, and she barely hesitated as she began hacking at one area of skin with her manicured thumb and finger nails. The soft flank flesh split after a minute of scraping and scratching, and a thin steady stream of blood trickled down and dripped onto the bed sheets. Mrs. Black held her free hand under the flow, catching as much blood as she could, and then brought her palm to her lips and drank. She licked the remaining blood from her hand and fingers and returned for more. When she had had enough to quench her thirst, she plugged the leak with a balled-up tissue from the box next to her side of the bed.

It was when she was reaching for the tissue that Mrs. Black noticed the book—one of her romances published by the same house that had printed the one she had been reading downstairs when her husband came home. She stretched for it, and finally got a hold of it by the bent cover. She had read it once before, two months earlier, but she used it now to pass the time, reading it over her husband's shoulder, awkwardly turning pages with her single bloodied hand. By the afternoon, when the heat rose and the flies returned—now tripled in number—she was so involved in the novel that she barely took notice.

The continuous summer heat made Mrs. Black faint-headed, and she lost track of how much time she had spent under her husband. Eventually she developed a routine. Each day she read the same book cover to cover, unplugged her husband's wound, made it bleed more, drank from the trickle of blood, and fell asleep as the bedroom cooled in the evening. Each day the flies multiplied. At first their rising numbers disturbed her as they flew and scurried everywhere— on the bed, on her husband, on her. She slowly got used to the ticklish sensation of them crawling all over her exposed flesh until, by the time they arrived one day (she had no idea which), she found she could ignore it and reread her book in peace. They didn't bother her again until later in the week, when the first of the maggots was born.

Mr. Black had grown increasingly ripe in the August heat. The stink had come on slowly at first, sneaking up on Mrs. Black, until one afternoon it rose thickly into the atmosphere of the room. Mrs. Black could not avoid it, but tried, turning her head every way she could manage. It was only in her effort, when she exhausted herself once more and began gasping, that she found some relief from the stench. From then on she was better, breathing through her mouth alone, not daring to sniff the air again. Yet even then she could still faintly taste the room overrun with decomposition.

The maggots had formed first behind Mr. Black's left ear—a ball of long wriggling worm-like creatures perched over Mrs. Black's face. They devoured her husband's flesh voraciously, tunnelling through his ear and into the softer food beyond. Sometimes a weaker member of the swarm would fall during the fight for sustenance and land on Mrs. Black's body. She would shake and wiggle as best she could, until the stray maggot fell out of her sight somewhere under her in the bed. Other packs grew during the following days or hours as well (Mrs. Black could not discern between the two by then)—in her husband's arm pit, between his buttocks, on the soles of his feet. When they started forming around the hole in his side, Mrs. Black was forced to make another from which to milk her husband.

Mr. Black rotted away on top of his wife for eight whole days before the smell became putrid enough for neighbours to notice and become concerned. On that eighth day, around ten o'clock in the morning, firemen were called to break down the door and find out what was happening. They discovered Mrs. Black, raving and insane, covered in maggots, flies, and the rotten flesh that used to be her husband. They pulled Mr. Black off of her then, and she could breathe freely at last. The rot poured from his eyes and nose and frozen grin as paramedics rolled him onto the floor and out of her sight. As Mrs. Black was draped in blankets and led to the ambulance that would take her someplace safe and clean, she did the last sane thing she could do given the circumstances.

She filled her lungs and laughed.

The Spare

I'M NOT GOING TO KILL YOU. I wanted to get that piece of information out in the open straight off so there's no misunderstanding—so you can be completely open and relaxed with me. You're going to survive this conversation. You're even going to be able to walk away on your own once we're done talking, you and me. Your life is in no danger, so put any thoughts of escape or running off out of your head and listen.

Now that you know your worst fears won't be realized, you should be able to focus with a clear mind. That's important, because you really need to hear what I have to say and understand it. This is about your life. Not about losing it because, as I said, that's not going to happen right now. If anything, this is a more serious threat. It's about you wasting your life.

You're on the wrong path, you see. I know it's a strange thing to hear coming from a man like me. I can hardly claim to be on the right path myself. I hurt people for a living. I'm not a hitman or an assassin. I'm what cops or reporters sometimes call an enforcer. I don't like to be called that. It sounds too formal. In the business, they sometimes call my sort a soldier, and I don't much care for that either. It makes my profession sound honourable, official, part of a noble collective, and it's sure not that. If I ever filed a tax return, and I was being honest—two big "ifs"—I'd write "thug" in the space they leave for you to state your profession. I'm a thug. I hurt people. Sometimes I hurt people so bad, they die. When that happens, it's usually on purpose, but I still wouldn't call myself a hitman or an assassin. I've met a few of them and those people are cold. People like that would never take the time out to have a conversation like we're having right now. So I guess you should be glad you're stuck talking to a thug. Believe me, in my world there are many people of few words you don't ever want to have to talk to.

You're young. You have your whole life ahead of you if you don't get too busy trying to shorten it. Lately you've been pissing off the wrong people. The sort of people who keep me on speed dial and pay me a monthly retainer to do what I do whenever they need me to do it. These people—and I'm sure you've already guessed who I'm talking about—wanted me to send you a message. Not like a memo, or a greeting card, or a love letter. These kinds of messages are expressed in broken bones and spilled blood.

Take it easy. I'm not going to get violent with you. I like you. Really, I do. So I want to make this as simple and painless as possible. For the both of us.

You see these? These are pruning shears. They're like little hedge clippers you use to trim bushes. Now you're going to hold still while I take a finger. Just one. And no, we're not going to argue about it. You see, it's important that you remember this conversation for the rest of your life. The longer you remember it, the longer that life will be. Think of this like that old trick of tying a string around your finger to remind you of something. It's just like that. Only the finger won't be there anymore.

There's a hospital just a few blocks away. Apply some pressure, try not to pass out, they'll fix you up fine. They could probably even reattach the finger, but they won't be doing that. I'll have to hold onto it, I'm afraid. You see, you're getting off light here. But the finger will serve as proof that I've done something to you. Something permanent. It's kind of like a receipt for the message I've delivered. You understand?

I knew you would. You're a real sport.

Let's begin.

Choke the Chicken

THE CARNIVAL, as it always did, as it always would, came to town. It was late in the spring, and the air was still cool. The snow was long gone, and the mud it left behind had had weeks to bake under the sun and transform into solid ground. Solid enough to pitch the tents that would house clowns and animal acts, and anchor the steel rides that would twirl and pitch and whip riders around with all sorts of nausea-inducing contortions. The setup was long and arduous, lasting days longer than it would cater to the public. When at last it opened its gates for business, the fair would spend a single weekend doing its very best to pick the pockets of everyone in town before packing up and moving to the next vacant field in its seasonal agenda.

Clive Whitworth had watched the tent peaks and the high rides slowly poke up over the town's modest skyline from his classroom window as the carnival was erected. The anticipation became unbearable as the weekdays dragged on, and Clive earned himself three separate detentions for ignoring his lessons in favour of gazing out the window. Such punishment had no effect on him or his carnival daydream. He only saw the extra half hours of after-school incarcerations as an opportunity to observe the distant construction from the slightly different vantage point offered by the windows of the detention room.

Although many of the other children in the school felt the same eager expectation for the weekend event, their interest was not aligned with Clive's. The enjoyment they derived from the attractions the annual carnival offered was more general, less focused. The fact was, Clive didn't particularly care for most of the spectacles that constituted a proper fairground. The rides made him sick, the candy floss gave him a belly ache. He didn't like clowns, and he cared even less for animals. What Clive liked was a challenge.

At long last, the school week dragged to its merciful end. It was late in the school year, and with the carnival in town, only a few of the most joyless teachers bothered to assign homework. None of them expected any of it to be done by Monday. In an otherwise dull town, this weekend would be a buzzing hive of entertainment options. No one would be wasting a single moment struggling through rudimentary algebra problems when there was so much fun to be had.

After a fitful night of sleep, Clive was up early. He could barely be convinced to finish his breakfast. Only the threat of withholding his allotment of fair money could keep him seated through his final bite of waffle and last strip of bacon. Once the go-ahead was finally issued by his parents, Clive threw on a light jacket and leapt from the front porch, dashing to the outskirts of town without ever stopping for breath or slowing his pace. He arrived at the wooden-placard gates of the carnival in eight minutes flat, beating his previous record by three. His growth spurt over the past year probably accounted for this, giving his legs an extra few inches of reach with each running stride.

The setup was nearly identical to the previous spring's and Clive remembered it well. Tickets for the rides and the shows could be purchased at a centrally located booth. Some shows cost one ticket, others two. The same went for the rides. The merry-go-round and the Ferris wheel, the tilt-a-whirl and the pirate ship, were all placed in their designated spots, spaced apart by the tents with the dancing dogs and the horse that could count. One strip along the border of the fairgrounds, stretching all the way from the funhouse to the haunted house, was where the carny booths were. Set in rows and forming an alleyway for games of chance and skill, they were ready to entrap anyone who dared navigate the gauntlet. Tickets wouldn't buy you a chance to win a stuffed toy here. Only cold hard cash could buy you a game. And the carnies would make sure you parted with a great deal of your cash before permitting you to walk away with a prize worth a fraction of what you spent to win it.

The lineup at the ticket booth was long and slow. Clive didn't care. He wasn't interested in tickets and didn't plan to purchase a single one. He was there for the games alley.

Clive considered himself a master of the games. He was undefeatable at the ring toss, always on target with a dart, air rifle or water pistol, and never failed to knock down a pyramid of cans with his three-ball allotment. Back home, stashed in a trunk in his closet, was his bounty from previous years. Plush pets, velvet posters, and plastic doohickeys of all sorts attested to his undeniable skill. He could have filled his entire room a dozen times over if his mother let him keep all the giant stuffed animals he'd won from the upper echelon of prizes. But they took up far too much space, and Clive had to admit they were garish, cheaply made, and filled with who-knows-what. One by one, he'd given them all up as they were pressed into service as gifts for birthdays and baby showers. He preferred to pore over his more compact collection of victories, often harder won. The prizes were all worthless junk, Clive was well aware, but to him they were more highly valued than mere money. They were testaments to his skill, well-honed through years of off-season practice.

Come carnival time, Clive would descend on the games alley and clean up. He would systematically travel from booth to booth, winning prizes, upgrading to bigger and better trophies, giving lesser ones away to friends who inevitably passed by on their way to the next ride or circus act. He wouldn't be satisfied until the carnies had all barred him from their individual booths for winning too much. That, to Clive, was the ultimate achievement, the one true prize he was really after. He'd made a clean sweep two years in a row now, banned for life from every single games booth. The lifetime ban was meaningless. The carnies never remembered him from year to year. They toured too many towns, saw too many faces. And Clive was still a growing boy. He hardly looked like the same kid who'd mopped the floor with them last year, or the year before.

Clive strolled the alley, checking out the games, watching the usual variety of unskilled marks lose their money as they missed their targets, failed to pop a balloon, or bounced a ball off the rim of what appeared to be an undersized non-regulation basketball hoop. The suckers. Clive had long ago figured out how all the games were rigged—how the odds were always stacked against the players like a crooked casino. He had also figured out how this gave him an unfair advantage, showing him the path to victory time and again. Practicing at home with some of his own roughly recreated challenges, he had vastly improved his skills, and had solved some of the trickiest deceits. The carnies always seemed to know how to win at their own games when they demonstrated to passersby how easy they were. Through observation and training, Clive had determined what sort of counter-intuitive backspin to give his ball throws, what sort of flick of the wrist could vastly improve his odds of landing a ring around a bottle neck, and where to aim an air rifle that had purposely had its sights miscalibrated.

The games were his to dominate. Clive's only question was where to begin.

"Are you smarter than The World's Smartest Chicken?"

This question was asked in bold red paint on an arched sign over a wheeled cart. On one side of the cart was a three-by-three grid of lights randomly flashing Xs and Os. On the other was a glass cage that held a disinterested-looking white chicken. The only other prominent feature on the cart was a coin slot, yawning open, eager to be fed. Clive had never seen anything like it before. Not at this fair, not anywhere. It was a confusing, alien addition to the landscape he'd memorized over the course of his gaming adventures.

One of the carnies selling three dart-throws at a wall of yellow, red and blue balloons observed Clive's long, thoughtful contemplation of the new attraction that had joined the alley this season. The carny was old, grizzled, a long-time veteran of the carnival and at least half a dozen just like it in years gone by. He knew a million ways to fleece the public out of the contents of their wallet, a dollar at a time if he could, a nickel at a time if he had to. But even in his advanced years, he was always open to learning a fresh approach. The World's Smartest Chicken was the latest trick up his sleeve. He'd been the loudest advocate for the chicken rig when one came on the market. It had been a tough sell to his fellow carnies, but none could denounce the benefit of a whole extra booth that didn't need to be manned by any additional employees and ran entirely on grain and a small amount of electricity. His argument won them over in the end and they all chipped in to buy it once they agreed to reap an equal share of its take.

The carny saw that curiosity had its hook in the boy.

"Give it a go, son. It won't bite," he encouraged. "Not tucked away behind that sheet of glass, it won't."

"How does it work?" Clive asked.

"It's tic-tac-toe. You know how tic-tac-toe works, don't ya?"

"Of course I do. But does the chicken?"

"Sure it does. Says it's The World's Smartest Chicken, don't it? You pop a dime in the machine and you play a game. If you beat it, well then, congratulations. If you tie it, then I guess you're only as smart as a chicken. And if you lose... Well, I wouldn't go telling anyone I'd lost a game of tic-tac-toe to a chicken, that's fer sure."

Clive's eyes fixed on the chicken behind the window. It didn't look any different from any other chicken he'd ever laid eyes on in his life. And out in his rural county, that amounted to a lot of chickens.

Almost unconsciously, Clive's hand slipped into his pants pocket and jingled the change nestled at the bottom. When he realized what he was doing, he removed his hand, only to find he'd come up with a single dime. This wasn't on his agenda, this uncharted attraction. Clive had a carefully calculated plan of attack. He knew which booths to hit first, which to hit last, and how long it would take him to work his way up to the top prize at each one. But this—this thing— stood in his way. There was no prize to be won, beyond the simple self-satisfaction of victory. Nevertheless, it stood as a barrier between him and his weekend loot. To ignore it, to circumvent it, would be to leave a challenge unanswered, and Clive wouldn't be able to return to school on Monday with his head held high if he had refused to meet it head-on.

He reached forward, slowly, deliberately, and pushed the dime into the coin slot. It rattled and clunked its way through the inner workings of the mechanism before landing in the coin bin at the bottom. The light board reset itself and the flashing Xs and Os vanished for the commencement of a new game. Inside the chicken's glass booth, a small trapdoor painted with the words "Thinking Booth" popped open on one of the walls. The chicken immediately rose to its feet, toddled over to the booth, and began pecking at the space hidden away behind the door. In response, a bold red X lit up on the board in the upper-left corner.

Clive saw that each square of the light board had a button so the human player could respond with his own move. He pushed the one next to the centre square, claiming it with a blue O.

Again the chicken pecked at its thinking-booth and another X appeared, this one in the bottom right. Clive countered with an O in the bottom left. The chicken knew enough to block him with an X in the upper right.

Only at this moment did Clive realize he'd made a rookie error. Even little kids playing tic-tac-toe with crayons on bits of scrap construction paper in kinder-garten knew better. You always play the corners in tic-tac-toe. It's not a sure way to win, but it's the only sure way not to lose. He'd left the chicken with two possible winning moves, and he could only block one of them.

Reluctantly, Clive chose one of his two blocks. With only one available move to win, the chicken seized it. The line of red Xs flashed victoriously, informing Clive he had lost. To his shame, he'd figured that out two moves ago. The question was, how did the chicken know?

"Tough break, kid," said the carny, who barely mustered enough politeness to keep from laughing out loud. "But like I said, that's one smart chicken."

Clive didn't respond, merely fumed. There was no recourse for the embarrassment but to dig into his pocket for another dime. To prove a point, he ran through a second match, quickly this time, playing the corners like he knew he should have from the start. The chicken once again played flawlessly, but with

Clive responding to each move correctly this time, the game finished in a mathematically certain tie. Clive wasn't able to defeat the chicken, but at least he'd proved he could hold it to a draw—world's smartest or not.

Clive turned back to the carny, prepared to flash him a cocky grin. But the carny had already turned his attention to another mark—a teenage boy with a girl at his side he was eager to impress. There might have been as much as ten dollars to be made off him before the teen won a fifty-cent teddy bear to gift to the girl. That was much more pressing business than goading some kid into losing a couple of dimes to a chicken.

With no more audience to prove himself to, Clive nearly took the opportunity to walk away and get on with his day. But one nagging question picked at his ego. He'd battled The World's Smartest Chicken to a draw, but could he defeat it? Against his better judgment, Clive dug for a third dime to feed into the coin slot.

And so the day went, slipping away minute by minute until the minutes accumulated into hours. Clive stood there as the sun crawled across the sky and the shadows grew long, pumping nickels and dimes into the coin slot, matching wits with a chicken and coming up short each time. Dissatisfied with tie after tie, Clive attempted a variety of strategies to unnerve the chicken and throw it off its game. He tried any number of nonsense moves in order to confuse and bamboozle his opponent. Each ploy to lull the chicken into a false sense of security failed, every attempt to lure it into a trap was evaded. The chicken displayed nerves of steel and kept to its purely logical game plan. The more outrageous and unpredictable Clive tried to be on the game board, the more losses he managed to rack up, until his tie-loss ratio versus his chicken nemesis started to become very embarrassing indeed. Not until many years later, when Kasparov matched wits with Deep Blue, did two such divergent masters butt heads so spectacularly.

The comparison was apt, for it was not a flesh-and-blood chicken Clive sought to defeat, but a machine— a machine built to do two things and two things only. Deceive and eat coins. The role Clive had unwittingly volunteered for was the dupe in a magic trick—a magic trick so simple, you didn't need a magician to perform it—just a rudimentary computer program and a hungry chicken. Each time it was the chicken's turn to move and the "Thinking Booth" swung open, the bird would quickly step over to peck at its unseen control panel, as though it were selecting which square it wanted to fill next. In fact, the only thing on the chicken's tiny mind was food. Conditioning had taught it that pecking at the inside of the booth would, at least once per match, open the grain dispenser in the cage, offering a rewarding snack. The truth was that no chicken, even The World's Smartest Chicken, could wrap its head around the complexities of tic-tac-toe. It just wasn't their thing. The humans outside the glass prison might as well be feeding spare change into a toll booth for all the chicken knew or cared. Any perceived human-chicken interaction was entirely one-sided.

Nevertheless, it was a good life as far as chickens are concerned, or at least better than most could look forward to. The cage was reasonably spacious, the food, though intermittent, was plentiful. And as an added bonus, the chicken got to humiliate humans by the dozen daily, which it might have appreciated had it a clue. On this particular day, however, there was only one obsessive human to humiliate. Clive hogged the machine until closing, only pausing for brief trips to the Port-A-Potties and to break his modest wad of saved dollars for more dimes and nickels at the hotdog kiosk.

When the announcement came over the PA speakers that the carnival was now closed for the day and customers needed to clear the grounds, Clive was dismayed to find he'd gone through his entire bankroll without a single win to his name.

Back home, Clive picked at his dinner, hardly eating anything, not really hungry anyway. When asked if he had fun at the carnival that day, he mumbled something grumpy and indistinct and then excused himself for an early bedtime.

After dark, once the rest of the house was asleep, Clive made the rounds. There remained another whole day to bounce back and salvage the season, but he needed to replenish his ammunition. Silently he raided his father's bill fold, his mother's change purse, and his little sister's penny jar. He knew the theft would not go undiscovered for long, but the consequences were something he'd only concern himself with come Monday morning, once the carnival was gone from town and out of his reach for another year. Until that moment, Clive's only thought was fixed on saving face, defeating the chicken once and for all, and moving forward with his original agenda to crush all the other games in the alley. There was still time if he moved quickly. A good night's sleep and a fresh start with a fresh perspective was all he needed. He'd come at the chicken hard in the first few minutes of the Sunday opening, catch it unawares before it had a chance to get up to speed, and then move on to a more deserving challenge.

Clive was absent at breakfast the next morning. It was the only way to be sure he was first through the gate the moment the carnival reopened for the day. He was at the chicken stand moments later, before any of the carnies had even assumed their positions in their game booths. He had to wait an additional ten minutes until someone came around to plug the cart into an extension that ran to one of the fairground's generators. Clive killed the time by staring coldly at his opponent, trying to rattle the chicken as it stared back with one profiled eye.

Once power was restored, Clive was lightning quick with his first coin. His money from the day before had all been removed overnight, and he could hear his first dime rolling on its rim once it dropped into the empty change bucket inside the machine. He was five dimes into the rematch before anyone else stepped foot in the arcade strip to man the booths or try their hand at the games. Clive played fast and decisively, hoping a sudden rapid assault of matches would afford him the advantage. Once again, Clive's strategy proved futile. A night's sleep had not improved his performance, and an early start had not thrown the chicken off its game.

After his late-night thievery, Clive had started day two with even more cash in his pockets. He went through it all twice as fast as he had previously and was bankrupt by noon. He spent the rest of the afternoon wandering the fairgrounds, hitting up any school friends he could find for spare change. He was able to borrow a few coins here and there. Close friends were willing to advance him as much as a dollar at a time. All of it was fed to the chicken in short order. Still hours away from the carnival calling it quits for the weekend, Clive was destitute. Word of his desperate fundraising had spread and no more loans were forthcoming. Even old pals turned their backs on him and hid, ducking behind thick queues of people, or losing themselves in the Hall of Mirrors, rather than get tapped by Clive again.

Any other year, even short on cash, Clive would have lingered and watched the rides and listened to the screams and laughter. But there was no joy left in it. He couldn't even bring himself to return one final time to the games in order to watch the unskilled lose their money at challenges he himself had mastered. Not with that damn superior chicken standing there, looking down on him from inside its glass box, all-seeing and all-knowing—at least in regards to anything tic-tac-toe related. Clive instead decided that it was time to return home, have something to eat at last, and face the consequences of his crime if it had been found out.

"Where were you this morning?" his mother wanted to know. When Clive didn't come down for breakfast, she had been every bit as worried as doting motherhood required her to be. But she had guessed exactly where her son was—the only place he could be—and had not called around or made inquiries of the neighbours.

"I wanted to get an early start," Clive shrugged.

"There's money missing. Do you know where it is?"

"Yeah," admitted Clive, and braced for the third degree, the disappointment, the punishment.

Sent to bed without supper, grounded for weeks' worth of home detention, Clive felt the sting of defeat weigh on him more heavily than any loss he'd ever experienced in his softball league or at a spelling bee. This was a loss that mattered, that haunted him. Sleep would not come, and he felt certain a peaceful slumber would never be his again until he purged this loss from his troubled mind. Slipping out of bed after the rest of the house was down for the night, pulling his clothes back on, Clive knew the hour was very late, but there was still time to catch the carnival before it skipped town. There he would have to face the chicken one final time.

Clive was not stupid so much as stubborn. He couldn't let things lie, not where they were. Winning was no longer on his mind. The sole focus of his every thought now was revenge. It would be quick and easy as killings went. He could picture his hands around the chicken's throat, squeezing tight, choking off its air supply, crushing bones, snapping its arrogant neck.

Would his midnight act of murder be investigated, traced back to him? Would charges be laid, prison time served? It was, after all, only a chicken. But this was The World's Smartest Chicken. Surely there would be a reckoning for such a special animal. Clive supposed it would depend on just how brilliant the chicken was—if tic-tac-toe was its sole talent, or if it offered more to the world. It had been undeniably brilliant anticipating Clive's every move so far. Did the chicken foresee this one as well? Would it raise an alarm, clucking and screeching for salvation before Clive could sneak up on it and commit the deed? Clive considered all this, but recognized he'd spent the better part of two days second guessing himself into this position. Best now to simply act, swiftly and brutally and with a violence no chicken could hope to match.

When he arrived at the fairgrounds, the tents were already flat on the ground and folded up. The staff was hard at work, tearing down all the temporary structures and packing the clapboards and canvas away in trailers that would be hitched to trucks and rolled to the next town in a matter of hours. The rides were still standing, steel skeletons, dark and imposing by moonlight. The power was out, the cables were being collected and spooled, and it was too dangerous to dismantle the big attractions in the dark. They wouldn't be torn down until morning, once all the lighter, more basic elements were out of the way and on the road.

The carnival workers toiled by flashlight and battery-operated lanterns. There was ample illumination for them to see what they were doing, but it was easy for one boy to slip by them unseen if he kept to the shadows. Clive's memory of the carnival layout helped him find his way in the dark without tripping over anything and calling attention to himself. It was a simple matter to find the games alley. The booths were empty now. Without their colourful prizes, blinking lights, bottles or balloons, they looked uniformly nondescript. The only stand in the strip that remained unique was the chicken's cart. The silhouette of its wagon-wheel spokes and the transparent glass cage stood out in the dim light that filtered through the grounds from the opposite end of the fair.

Clive could see the chicken sitting inside its cage, unaware of his presence. He approached the cart, looking for a latch that would open the glass box and allow him access to his enemy—a clear path to a neck that needed wringing. He ran his fingers around the frame, feeling for the mechanism, but found nothing. It was too dark to see how the box was opened. Clive considered shattering one of the panes, ramming his elbow through it, hoping not to cut himself too severely. But that would alert the workers, rouse the chicken, remove the advantage of surprise. He tried to calculate whether or not he would have enough time to get his fingers around the throat of a panicked and alarmed chicken before rescue was at hand.

Clive was still considering his options when he felt something underfoot. It was an extension cord. He reached down and hooked it with a couple of his fingers. Following it along its path, he arrived at a multi-socketed plug that rested at the end of a larger power line near one of the empty booths. Perhaps he could risk a little light to find his way in the dark, thought Clive. It might go unquestioned by the busy men long enough for him to accomplish the assassination and slip away unnoticed.

Clive plugged in the chicken cart and the tic-tac-toe board lit up. Reset, the game blinked twice and then defaulted into automatic mode. No one was feeding change into the coin slot, but tic was matched against tac in a brutal duel that ended in stalemate each time. Clive could see that it wasn't the chicken playing at all. The machine was playing itself. And there was something else he noticed by the light provided by the red and blue Xs and Os.

The chicken was brown.

"Who's that?" said a gravelly voice from behind one row of wooden stands. It was the old carny from the dart-toss—the one who had baited Clive into challenging the genius chicken. Clive's first instinct, having been discovered trespassing, was to flee. He fought the impulse, determined to seek answers instead.

Clive walked around the left flank of the games alley to address the carny directly. There was a small campfire burning behind the stands, with several wooden crates pulled up next to it. The carny was seated on one, warming himself over the modest blaze that had been invisible from the alley.

"What happened to The World's Smartest Chicken?" asked Clive.

The carny pointed at the chicken in the rig through a narrow gap in the alley's wooden façade. It remained nestled, eyes closed, dozing for the night.

"You're looking at it, kid."

"That's not the same chicken as before."

The carny considered the chicken currently residing in the glass cage, then returned his attention to the spit that was set up over the camp fire. He'd been cooking up some fowl for his dinner before the boy interrupted.

"No, I guess that makes this one the new world-champ."

"I don't get it? Did it beat the other chicken in a match or something?"

"You could say that," nodded the carny, tearing away a strip of greasy skin from the roasted bird's plucked breast as it sizzled over the open flame. "It wasn't no tic-tac-toe match, though. It was more of a taste test."

The carny cackled slightly to himself as he popped the loose skin into his mouth and sucked at the tips of his fingers where he'd just been holding it.

Clive noticed a small pile of discarded white feathers behind the games-alley backdrop. A slight nighttime breeze played with them, scattered them in random directions. They'd all be blown away by tomorrow, gone like the rest of the carnival.

"You want a drumstick?" asked the carny, tearing one of the tender legs off his meal and offering it to the boy.

Clive remembered the stories he'd heard of tribes in the deepest darkest jungles of the world. Some of them would eat their defeated enemies as a way to imbue themselves with their strength, their power. It was both a sign of respect for their fallen foes, and a way of stealing all they ever were and making it their own. Clive had thought that sounded kind of dumb when he first heard about it. But the way he saw things and the way he thought about them kept changing the more living he got under his belt. These days he wasn't so sure about much of anything. He wasn't even sure if that much uncertainty in life frightened or excited him.

"Yeah," he said, and sat down to eat.

The Appeal

SHEFTON WAS ENTERING the third year of his stretch. The only person he ever saw from outside the walls was his lawyer—scheduled visits all, set in advance, at regular times and intervals. So when he was told he had a visitor on a Saturday afternoon in October, he knew it wasn't his lawyer. There was only one person on earth it could be.

"How's the sardine can look from the inside?"

Shefton had been sitting on the stool, looking through the thick Plexiglas at his guest and holding the phone receiver to his ear for a full minute before Reggie spoke. Apparently they still had words to say to each other after thirty years of friendship and five more of bitter rivalry. This fact surprised both men equally.

"I never expected you to come visiting."

"And yet you put me on your visitor list."

"I got no family left," Shefton reminded Reggie of the fact neither man could ever forget. "Figured I had to put somebody. So what are you doing here? I thought you'd still be sore."

"I am," said Reggie. "But I have some legal advice I wanted to pass on to you."

"You a lawyer now?"

Reggie ignored the sarcasm. Visiting time was limited, and there was a point that needed getting to.

"You have an appeal in the works. Looking pretty good. Very promising with the inadmissible evidence and such."

"I'm told it's got a good chance."

"Drop it," Reggie told him.

"Fuck you, drop it. I already done two years. I ain't looking forward to eighteen more. Even with time off for good behavior."

"About that."

"Yeah?"

"After you drop the appeal—if, some years down the road, you find yourself in front of a parole hearing, I want you to chat them up about how you can't wait to get out so you can reoffend."

"Why in the hell would I do any such thing?"

"Because you need to do the whole life sentence."

"You have any idea how old I'll be if I do all my time?"

The two men didn't know each other as children. They first met when they were already young men— up and coming career criminals with a checkered past

behind them and a spotty future in front. Nevertheless, they'd grown up side-by-side in all the ways that
count—bonded by blood and profit, divided by those
same things. They were getting on now, and would
never grow old together.

"I can work out the figures, yeah. Twenty years.
Do them all. Every day of it. I mean it. We're mates.
We go back. We're like brothers, you and me. And
when you get out, I'm going to kill you, I swear it."

Reggie didn't need to make it an oath. Shefton
knew he meant it, and had already assumed as much.

"I don't want to do it, but I will on principle and
you know my reasons," continued Reggie. "In here, I
can't touch you. Sure, I could pay for some lifer ape to
shiv you in the showers, but I've always prided myself
on doing my own killing. It's what separates us from
those shits who get somebody else to do their dirty
work."

Shefton said nothing. Nothing needed saying. They
both knew those shits well, had slaved for them for
years, and had killed for them too many times to
count.

"So while you're in here," said Reggie, "you're safe
from me and I don't have to do what needs doing. I
figure if we're both lucky, the kind of life I lead might
get me killed before your twenty years are up and then
you won't have to worry about coming back out into
the world."

Reggie let Shefton sit in silence for a moment before asking, "So how about it? Can you do this for me?"

"I'll talk to my guy," said Shefton at last. "Maybe he hasn't filed the papers yet. He won't like it."

"You could explain the situation to him."

"No, I couldn't."

Reggie nodded. Neither man could. Some personal histories are too complicated to explain to an outsider—the time spent together, the layers of betrayal once it all went wrong. Who could ever understand if they hadn't lived it?

Shefton took his time walking back to his cell. He hadn't seen Reggie face-to-face in years, but it was like no time had passed. Making an enemy of him had been the hardest thing he ever had to do in his life. It was good to know, even with all the hatred between them now, that his best friend was still looking out for him. Was that worth another eighteen years of his life? The rest of his days in a concrete cage?

Considering it was the only thing left of his old life outside, yeah. Maybe it was.

Meridian Response

THE SLEEP MASK goes on first, even though I won't be napping. Then it's the noise reduction headphones, even though I'm alone, the room is silent, and any outside traffic noise is remote. Once it's quiet and dark, I raise one eye of the mask long enough to click on my new audio file. Then I lie back in my armchair and do nothing but breathe and listen as the soothing sounds take hold of me and I feel the tingle run through my whole body.

They call this experience ASMR because everything is an acronym these days. The technical term is autonomous sensory meridian response. I just think of it as my moment. It's a common enough response to certain gentle sounds. Most people who experience it get triggered by whispering, and there are plenty of files to be had online for those so inclined. Gigabytes of men and women talking sweet nothings in hushed voices—everything from the utterly mundane, to the outright pornographic, even though ASMR isn't supposed to be about sex. Other sounds do it for different people. Some like to hear the tide lapping at a shore. Wind is another popular one, with or without chimes. You can listen to paper being crumpled for hours on end if that's your preference, or ice cubes cracking and melting in a glass of water.

I've tried them all, but none of them do it for me. I'm a very niche audience. But if you look long enough, if you stretch the search engines to their limits and poke around the dark web, you'll find your niche in the end. No matter what you're into, there's a community out there waiting for you. A simple email, polite and inquisitive, and they'll send you everything you're looking for, hoping their generosity will one day be reciprocated with a fair trade. In any case, they'll be delighted to find a kindred spirit, a closeted fetishist, a fellow freak. And they'll be eager to share.

It's almost like hearing a zipper being unzipped. That first incision is always the best, and it pulls me right into the experience immediately. Two more incisions, shorter and more to the point, follow. Then there's the great peeling back of the flesh. Skin, muscle and fat spread their wings like a great bird, exposing the next act of the show. The juicier it sounds, the better. I can usually tell by then how sloppy and gooey things are likely to get and I'm lost in the zone. You could set the room on fire and I probably wouldn't notice.

The recording is a quality one, made especially for my market. It wasn't for trade or file share like most of the others. This one cost me a bank transfer to the anonymous source, but it was well worth it. I can hear everything down to the gentle clinking of the surgical instruments as they come into contact with each other inside the body cavity, or are returned, wet and spent, to the steel tray.

Official recordings are never as good. The medical examiner will be making notes as his work progresses. Numbers are dictated as organs are weighed one by one, and contusions are diligently noted, along with any other irregularities. When it's a suspicious death, they hardly shut up long enough for me to hear the good parts. Some of my fellow audiophiles are okay with the chatter, but I find it too distracting. Such sessions are only worth it for the closing moments, once the cause of death has been ascertained, and all that's left to do is quietly stitch up the damage. If they take their time, I can achieve some certain degree of rest and relaxation, but my shot at that euphoric full-body buzz is ruined.

It was sheer happenstance that allowed me to discover how the subtle sounds of an autopsy affected me. It's not like I work in a morgue or a funeral home or any other place you might be expected to hear that scintillating moment when a sharp object first pierces and cuts open human flesh. I came to know what I was looking for because I remembered the first time I felt that delicious tingling sensation run across my scalp and down my neck. It only lasted for a few moments, but it made an impression.

I found what would become my recreational rapture in high school of all places. Most kids that age are discovering puberty and new hair growth. I chanced upon my sensory muse.

It was thanks to one student I didn't even know, who was obviously having a bad day. In a moment of acute frustration over some adolescent turmoil, he lashed out, punching one of the windows in a stairwell door. The window was built to take abuse, with a net of metal mesh inside the glass itself. But the blow of an angry young man who had yet to discover his own strength was enough to break through, and his fist came out the other side of one frame, along with a small explosion of glass fragments.

The student immediately withdrew his arm from the shattered window, not thinking, frightened by what he'd done and the trouble he'd get into for doing it. I was close enough to hear the shards dig into his flesh and tear through his skin, all the way down his forearm. The cuts were deep and hit an artery along the way. That long resonance of splitting tissue was followed by a soft pitter-patter of dollops of blood falling to the floor. The kid had his hand over his wound in an instant, realizing what had happened. Covered, the severed artery couldn't squirt, but instead dribbled like a tap, punctuating one compelling sound with another. I felt dizzy and probably looked like I would faint, but it wasn't the sight of blood making me ill, it was a heady bliss induced by the auditory assault of the moment.

The kid ran right past me, with a surprisingly calm, "Look out!" He beelined to the school office, seeking medical assistance. An ambulance was summoned, and I heard it was the biology teacher who kept the bleeding under control and saved the student's life, even as he fought to keep his lunch down. I lost my appetite as well, but it was due to my mind being elsewhere, replaying the noises from the incident, trying to select and remember the ones that had made me feel so calm and centred when everyone else who witnessed the accident was panicking.

A PBS documentary about forensic pathology years later would set me on the path to hunt for autopsy recordings. I already knew surgery scenes didn't do anything for me—too many people in the room with bleeping monitors and life-support clutter. But the lonely vigil of the solitary autopsy—that was promising. That particular television program was of no use, showing limited footage of the procedure, and spoiling the audio by removing it entirely and replacing the natural sounds with asinine narration. But it gave me an idea of where I could find the stimuli I craved, and how I could recreate the sensations I had once felt at a vulnerable age.

Recorded sound works for a quick fix, but nothing compares to being in the room for the real thing. It took a long time, but through arranged meetings, contrived friendships, and straightforward bribes, I've managed to cultivate connections with a few coroners and medical examiners locally and in neighbouring cities. For the right price, they'll occasionally let me sit in on an autopsy. The conditions are very strict, of course. I can't touch anything, which is fine because I don't want to—my needs aren't tactile. It has to be a routine autopsy that isn't expected to be part of any criminal investigation. And it can only be at night, when no one else is around, particularly any sort of supervisor or higher authority.

They think I'm weird, of course. All I do is sit in a chair with my eyes closed, out of the way, but near enough to the table so I can hear every nuance of what they're doing. Because these aren't criminal cases, I can usually get away with a request for no talking. Rather than reporting their findings into a microphone hanging over their workspace, they'll accept a monetary bonus to scribble their findings onto a notepad instead. That offers me the best results, and I'm so lost in my own head at the end of it, they often have to shake me by the shoulder an hour or so later to tell me it's time to leave.

The only loud noise I'm good with is the climactic Stryker saw, used to cut off the bowl of the skull so the brain can be removed, examined and weighed. It's the only electric instrument typically used in an autopsy. You might think such a cacophony would draw me out of the moment, but I find it quite thrilling. Since the ASMR tingling sensation begins and is most intense in my scalp, I feel an extra kinship with the rotating blade as it relentlessly hacks its way through solid bone, right in the same vicinity. I always request this be done last, with the subsequent squishy sounds of grey matter being manhandled serving as dessert to a fine aural dinner.

You could say it's an addiction, like a drug. I can't get enough. And like an addict, I've been chasing a bigger and better fix in an effort recreate that perfect first high. It's why I came up with the plan—the plan to reach my ultimate meridian.

I know I can't rely on any of my usual contacts. My increasing demands have pushed my luck with most of them. When I broached the subject with my top cutter, he threw me out and told me to never come back. That's one bridge burned, but it's okay. After this next delectable sensory buffet, I won't need anyone else's services again.

● ● ●

Assuming none of the others will want anything to do with this next step either, I take my search abroad, where life is cheap, and my dollars are worth so much more. The expected weeks of preparation turn into months, but I'm so excited about this adventure, I barely listen to any of my tapes anymore. Before long, I've practically gone cold turkey. Everything else pales in comparison to what I'm lining up. Finally, I'm ready to pack a bag and take the trip of a lifetime. As I get off a connecting flight with no return ticket, I know my goal is close.

A few people question me about my travel destination. Why the hell would anyone vacation in a semi-failed state that was so recently a war zone? No one who works at customs on the other side of my journey cares though, and that's all that matters. They aren't going to deny access to any dumb tourist willing to feed their broken economy. I willingly tell them about the travellers cheques I'm bringing into the country with me. A cursory inspection of my luggage fails to discover the stack of foreign cash I have stuck in my spare socks. Those are the holiday funds I neglect to tell them about for fear of racking up some impromptu airport "fees." They let me pass with a final stamp in my passport, and a visa to stay for a maximum of six months. I don't expect to stay for more than six hours.

The world is full of goons who will hurt a person of your choice for money—even the one paying the shot, if that's their thing. But I don't want a knee-breaking thug or a sicko with a pair of brass knuckles. I need a specific sort of professional—skilled, trained, with years of experience and the proper equipment.

An airport taxi takes me straight to the hospital, even though it's been closed for two years following a direct missile hit. There's only one person waiting there for me. He used to be on staff, but the doctors and nurses are all gone. So are the patients who survived the blast. There are others still lost under the collapsed wing. Their remains might be excavated and properly buried one day, once the military has finished excavating the landmines and unexploded ordnance that litter the sector.

The man hasn't been back in many months and wouldn't be here now if I weren't paying him. His salary was cut off before the hospital even got hit, and he tells me about the family he needs to feed, like I have to excuse him for his sins to come.

This former technician leads me through the nearly deserted hospital. We hear the occasional clatter echoing through the corridors, which might only be a rat, but could just as easily be a homeless refugee or worse. He seems nervous, but I urge him on. I don't expect to find anyone squatting where we're going. Even people desperate for shelter will opt for just about any other roof over their head before they resort to a morgue.

A couple of battery-operated lanterns guide us to the basement. Once we've locked ourselves in the barren room, there are still enough intact white tiles on the wall to reflect the light back at us and brighten the place to an acceptable level. I throw down my lone carry-on bag and retrieve the wad of cash, leaving it on a counter where my hired hand can see it. It's not the national currency, which hyperinflated and collapsed with the onset of war. The sight of greenbacks seals the deal and I shamelessly strip naked right in front of him.

Ever since I found and retained this unemployed medical examiner, he's been making preparations, confirming that the tools of the trade were still on site—that they hadn't been looted and sold for scrap. I see he's rigged a battery pack that was charged elsewhere and then relocated here to wait for us. The top priority is the drugs, which were begged, borrowed, and stolen from half a dozen dentists, most of them also out of work and destitute. I'd been able to get him enough cash through the mail in dribs and drabs to make it all happen. A single bill or two, folded into a couple of sheets of instructions, could avoid being spotted and pilfered during the circuitous route to his doorstep. Now that I'm here, I can pay him the balance with more cash money than I'd dare risk to a dysfunctional and corrupt postal system.

I lie down on the steel table, pointing my feet towards the sloping end. It's cold and dusty and not the least bit sanitary, but that doesn't matter. Soon enough, I'll be numb to everything but the ambient sound of the sealed chamber.

I don't want to be distracted by pain, and that's what the analgesics are for. I opt for enough novocaine to cripple a horse without causing drowsiness because it's important I stay awake and aware. The tiny needles, hundreds of them, hurt. Every single one is an irritating pin prick, often in very sensitive places, until each new one becomes its own torture.

That's fine. I'll take the pain now so I'm able to concentrate during the procedure later.

After each round, he pokes me in a few spots to see if I can feel anything. If I can, he doses me again. If I can't, he moves to inject the next spot. He works quickly. This all needs to be over before the first shots start to wear off.

It takes about fifteen minutes before we're ready for the initial incision. He asks me if I'm sure. I close my eyes and tell him I am. Then we begin.

He starts at my breast bone, nearly at my throat, and pierces the skin with a scalpel that's still razor sharp after years of neglect. I can barely hear it enter, but once he drags it down my chest, off the rib cage, and through my belly, almost to the groin, I sigh contentedly. It's a sound I've heard many times before, but never so close, never so intimately. It's just what I wanted.

Two more incisions stretch from my collar bones and join the first long cut, creating the contours of a window that will be opened to expose my internal organs. I don't feel a thing. My nerves are deadened in all the spots where the cuts are scheduled to happen. The only sensation I can feel is the blood cascading down either side of my body, pooling under me, and streaming towards the drain at my feet. This is, after all, a vivisection, not an autopsy, and I still have a beating heart to pump blood. So long as he doesn't hit any major blood vessels, I'll have enough left in me to see this through.

Peeling the flesh back, he slices at the underside, where skin still clings to bone, helping it along. This is everything I hoped it would be. Even doped up on local anesthetics, nerves unresponsive, I feel the tingle where it counts. It's in my mind, and it's never been better. Once I'm opened up, his rubber-gloved hands play around my exposed organs as I've instructed him, just so I can hear the wetness, the viscosity. There's only so much novocaine can accomplish, and I can't have him go digging as deep as I'd like, spooling out intestines, removing kidneys, bisecting my liver. Those are all organs that can experience pain, and I'm only able to suffer a certain level of discomfort without drawing myself out of my aural ecstasy.

Luckily, there's one internal organ that can take the abuse, and we've saved the best for last. Once he's cut me to ribbons, it's time to crack out the charged battery. Having done his worst with forceps and scissors, it's the bone saw's turn to have a taste. A hear the familiar whirl of the Stryker blade and feel it tear through my needle-tracked scalp. There's no pain at all, only an intense vibration as he orbits my skull, just above the ears, from temple to temple and then across my brow. When he pulls the bowl off, it sounds so much like a ripe melon being opened, I momentarily feel hungry.

The brain is what processes input from the rest of the body, but the organ itself isn't subject to physical pain. It doesn't have the nerves to detect damage first hand. I'm aware of him cutting into the liquid sack around the lobes now, but I can't feel the expected agony of him freeing them from their nest, scooping my entire cerebellum right out of the bony cavity that was supposed to keep it safe. The slashing, the scraping, the tugging sensation—it's an exquisite violation. I focus on it for as long as I can, savouring my final sensations, my last luscious sensory input, my meridian moment before the damage being done makes it impossible to process the keepsake balloon edifice caltrop advice...

Drain plug algorithm burlap...
Swim butter tip...
Po...

...

Young Turks
and Old Wives

THE APARTMENT TOWER sticks out of the neighbourhood like a single broken tooth. Chipped white
concrete exposes the rusty checkerboard rebar just
under the surface. If somebody doesn't condemn the
building, it'll fall down all on its own one day. Sooner
rather than later, fingers crossed. A pile of rubble
would be less of an eyesore. Wipe that fuck-ugly
building off the map and the money would still be left
standing. The money wouldn't go away. It would find
another dark corner to go hide in, like the rats and the
cockroaches.

It's the first of the month which means rain or
shine, shit or storm, I have to get my ass down there
to cook the books. They send a car around to pick me
up at my house. It's not that they don't trust me to
show up on time, it's that I don't trust that hellhole to

leave my car alone for a ten-minute appointment. This is one of my conditions. The other is that they send a respectable looking driver in a respectable looking vehicle. No gangstas in a muscle car, hopping around on hydraulics and jacked up on blow. What would the neighbours say?

Today it's a new guy and a new car, both acceptable. The car is luxury but non-descript, the driver sharply dressed, also non-descript. We don't bother with introductions. It's not important we know each other's name so long as we know where we fit in with the organization.

"You new?" is all I ask him.

He's too mature, too well dressed, carries himself too well, to be new talent. But I haven't seen him around before. He's either from out of town, or operates locally in circles I have no personal contact with.

"Not really," is as much explanation as I get from him. It suits me. We listen to the radio instead of making small talk.

Half an hour later, we're in another world. Urban sprawl gives way to urban blight, and finally urban apocalypse. This is the part of town the degenerates and lowlifes look down their noses at. Nobody comes here unless they're looking to score, and nobody stays longer than it takes to get well. Even the hard-core junkies, jonesing for a fix, will wait until they're clear of the area and among a better class of scumbag before they shoot up.

We pull alongside the curb and I have to look through the sunroof to see the top floors. Thanks to some zoning kickbacks decades earlier, it's the only tower for blocks. Once upon a time, somebody wanted to build a high-rise and paid the necessary bribes down at city hall to make it happen. Maybe they thought it would be catching, that urban renewal would spread like a virus. They didn't realize the whole neighbourhood was already terminal.

In a dodgy corner of town, the tower was gleaming and modern for the first few years. But it was cheaply built, badly maintained, and by the end of its first decade of existence, it was such a dump it looked like it had been standing there as long as all the century-old tenements it dwarfed. When it was repurposed as something known locally as The Factory many years later, all those levels were put to good use. These days there's a meth lab on seven. The coke-cutters are on nine. Stolen brand-name meds are packed and distributed throughout three and four. Homemade pills are milled out on five and six. Everything is nicely compartmentalized on a floor-by-floor basis.

Eleven through fourteen serve as a grow-op jungle of pot plants and sun lamps. The windows are painted black to keep the place from shining like a lighthouse beacon all night long. Extension cords run across telephone poles and plug into neighbouring buildings to help distribute the energy demand, but the lamps suck up so much juice the electric company has to know they're feeding a mary-jane greenhouse. And if they know, the cops know. But a raid has never materialized. Cops like a toke of quality weed just like the next guy, and who wants to fuck up a good thing? Through hassle or hustle, one way or the other they all get their piece once the goods hit the street. Nobody is willing to step up, make an arrest, and become the most hated boy scout in the troop.

Or maybe the cops just don't want a high-profile drug collar to turn into an even higher-profile blood-bath. The lobby of the building is always thick with lookouts. There's never a shortage of young men willing to keep an eye out for a small cut of the take and a taste of the wares. Paranoid and packing, they're itching for a fight that might be coming with every strange face that walks down the street, every unfamiliar car that drives past their block.

We pass one of the boys on the way inside. I know him by his ink, but I can't remember the name. He's standing at the base of the building with a long rubber hose running back to a tap inside. The way he's spritz-ing the landscape, he looks like a gangbanger gone straight, trying to care for his lawn in some upwardly mobile suburban bliss. The problem is there's not a hint of grass in sight and it ruins the effect.

"Trying to grow a garden of weeds between the cracks?"

"Boss is doing some spring cleaning around here."

There's a dark patch on the concrete where he's been hosing it down. The water running into the gutter still hints at a pinkish-red colour. Somebody probably got shot. Somebody probably got dead. Ambulances won't come here. Nobody will call 911. If you get shot or beaten badly enough, you'd better be able to drag yourself to a hospital. Nobody will lift a finger to get you help while you're alive, but they'll all lend a hand to make sure your body disappears if you die on the premises.

"Looks like somebody had a bad day," is my comment.

"A lot of somebodies are having a bad day today," he says.

"And here you are, mopping up the mess."

"Cleaning up is a dirty job."

"That's profound," I told him. "You should write that one down. Stuff it in a fortune cookie."

"Fuck you."

"These kids," I tell my driver as we head for the front door, "None of them know how to take a compliment."

"Maybe you don't sound sincere."

"I said it with a smile."

"Accountants don't do sincere smiles."

Over the life of the building, low-rent housing for the poor had become a no-rent factory for the 82nd street drug cartel. Not to be confused with the 83rd street drug cartel, the boys on 82 are big time, dealing a little of everything in the recreational-narcotics spectrum. Their vast empire spans all the way back to 79th street and the two blocks bordered by boulevards north and south. That comes to nearly five and a half square blocks where they own the exclusive rights to deal to every degenerate who juices, shoots or puffs on that postage stamp of concrete. As a client base goes, it's a good whack of addicts who have decided to call the neighbourhood home—or at least decided it was a good enough place to get high, piss their lives away, overdose and die. There's money to be made. Not a huge amount—there's only so much a bunch of late-stage terminal junkies can steal to support their habit—but it all belongs to the cartel.

Inside we're met by more of the hired help. The day watch, same as the night watch, fuelled by a speedball cocktail of cocaine and heroin, lubricated by half-sugar, half-caffeine energy drinks that are designed to keep you up and burn you out. Most of the boys have been awake for days. Their version of down time is a burgers-and-fries snack and a 48-hour coma on one of the bare mattresses in the building's former laundry room. Then it's back to the vigil and a fresh shot of junk to keep them wide-eyed and aware like a good guard doggie—paranoid and suspicious of everything, ready to bark at a passerby and bite an intruder.

I run my own laundry room, only mine doesn't house a bunch of stressed and stoned lookouts trying to grab a nap between hits. The work I do for the cartel—and a select few other gangs—is to turn their ill-gotten proceeds into legit numbers in a bank account. I count the money, crunch the numbers, wave my magic accounting pen, and turn it all into taxed,

legal and unquestioned tender. Oh, they keep plenty
of piles of cash on hand to throw around and play at
being big men in a small neighbourhood. But paper
piles up, and nobody wants to leave too much money
stacked around the workplace. Even crooks get
robbed. And the top guys are bright enough to plan
for the future. What good is profit if you can't spend it
on a nice car, a nice house, or a high-yield dividend
stock to see you through your retirement if you ever
live that long? You can't buy these things with cash-
on-hand unless you want a visit from John Law.

So I make the money look good by running it
through a series of businesses. I've brokered the sale
of a number of fronts at bargain prices. Currently, the
cartel is the proud owner of a restaurant nobody ever
eats at and a bar nobody ever drinks at. Then there's
the long-term storage facility that only stores row
upon row of empty lockers. They have two dance
clubs downtown. One of them never opens its doors,
the other never shuts them because the place is gutted
and full of pigeons and pigeon shit. There's also the
landmark movie theatre that hasn't shown a movie
since colour was a novelty and the debate raged on
whether talkies were here to stay. On paper it's a
community centre, even though no one from the
community has seen the inside of the place since it
was boarded up twenty years ago with placards that
announced "Under renovation" and "Opening soon."
Failed businesses all, but in the books they're gold
mines. If you tell the tax man your dive bar is the

hottest watering hole in town, he'll just cash your cheque and congratulate you. You think he gives a shit it's all drug money? Of course not. So long as you can produce enough fake numbers to convince him you're not guilty of tax evasion, he doesn't care what else you might be guilty of.

There's a fire burning in the lobby. No fireplace, just a fire. Trash is being burned in a garbage can in the middle of the floor so the watch dogs can keep warm. With so many broken windows, the place gets drafty. I'd be concerned about an open blaze setting off the fire alarm or the sprinklers, but none of that equipment has worked in years.

When my driver and I get closer, I can hear the boys talking tall tales. With nothing better to do than get high and tell each other work-related anecdotes, they can always be counted on for a good story or two when I visit. I might as well be witnessing primitive man from a hundred thousand years ago, telling ghost stories over camp fires. The ghost stories change, the fuel burning in the pit changes, but man remains primitive, superstitious. Savage and fearful.

I linger, so my driver stops to listen too. "Skiff" is what they call the scrawny collection of bones and needle tracks who has the floor. He recognizes me from my monthly visits and nods a greeting. Skiff is always there, always on watch, always ready with a story. Every first of the month I experience the same mild surprise that he's still alive, still bullshitting. But he'll outlive the building, that Skiff. Like the rats and the cockroaches and the money, Skiff will go on.

"Stop me if you've heard this one before," he says.

We're all heard this one before, but nobody stops him.

"This one time, Dunlan's in an elevator. Derek Dunlan, right? You've heard of him. Everyone's heard of him. He's in an elevator and it's packed. No room to breathe, no room to slouch, people are standing shoulder-to-shoulder. Everybody's in everybody else's personal space, got it? And then the elevator stops. Dead. Power failure, or it just breaks down, or something. It's not important. Just know that this motherfucker isn't going anywhere anytime soon. People bitch, people complain, but not our Dunlan. He just stands there, quiet, doesn't say shit. He closes his eyes like he's going to sleep or meditating or some damn thing and he's a statue. Meanwhile everybody else is freaking out. Slow at first. Situation like that, you want to stay calm, be polite, be considerate of your fellow man. Whatever. But after ten, twenty minutes, folks get antsy. After an hour they're going fucking nuts. The air's stale, everybody's sweating, it's hot like a sonofabitch. And this is what happens.

"One guy lights up. I don't know if he's claustrophobic, or a nic addict, or just a miserable fucking asshole, but he takes out his pack of cigarettes and lights one. People complain. Obviously. Shit like, 'You're not allowed to smoke in here,' or 'We can hardly breathe as it is.' And he's all like, 'Fuck you! I need this!' And people shut up because they don't know if the guy's a freak or not. But our Dunlan has something to say. Understand now, Dunlan's been quiet as the dead. He hasn't said a word the whole time. He hasn't moved or opened his eyes in about an hour. Hell, he's not even sweating. But now he opens his eyes and says very calmly, very politely, 'Please put that out.'

"The guy puffing away, I don't know what he says. Maybe he gives Dunlan another 'Fuck you,' or maybe he doesn't have anything to say. Bottom line, though, is that he's still smoking. So Dunlan tells him, still calm, but a little less polite, 'Put it out, or I'll put it out for you.'

"This time I'm sure the smoker gives Dunlan a 'Fuck you' or worse. Whatever he said, a second later he's screaming. And I mean screaming his head off worse than you've ever heard anyone scream in your life. Because Dunlan leaps across the elevator. There's nowhere to move, but suddenly everybody just somehow finds room to get the fuck out of his way. The sardines part like the Red Sea and Dunlan's all over the guy. He lets him have a knee in the groin to give him something to think about, and before anyone knows what's happening, he's got the guy's head jammed in the corner of the car. With one hand he's forcing the guy's eye wide open, with the other he takes the cigarette from his mouth and stubs it out right in his eyeball. And none too fast either. He lets it simmer there for a bit. And that's when the screaming starts and it just keeps going and going, even after Dunlan lets the guy drop and flicks the dead butt at him.

"So Dunlan goes back to exactly where he was standing and assumes the position like nothing happened. Everyone's too stunned to say dick. And even if they had anything to say, no one would have heard it because smoker-boy is still screaming himself horse. Dunlan lets this go on for a little while, but it only takes him about a minute to have had his fill of that shit. So he just says all soft spoken, 'Quiet please.'

"Nothing. The guy's still screaming like he didn't hear, which is probably the case. So Dunlan repeats himself, 'I said, quiet please.' And the smoker must have heard that one because he says something back. 'You burned my fucking eye out!' which is stating the obvious, but at least it's a little more articulate than all that hollering. And Dunlan just tells him, cool as a cucumber, 'You saw what I did to make you stop smoking. You don't want to see what I'll do to you to make you stop shouting.' And that does the trick. The guy shuts the fuck up in a big hurry, but then some other people in the elevator start thinking they can talk shit to Dunlan. Maybe they figure he's just one guy and they outnumber him. Who knows, but one big guy right behind Dunlan thinks he's got balls.

"'You're a fucking psycho,' the big guy says. And Dunlan turns around to look this guy right in the face. He's stares at him, not hard or mean or anything. He just stares at him, indifferently, like he's watching paint dry. And you can practically see this other guy shrinking. He doesn't know where to put his eyes, so he tries to out-stare his shoes. And Dunlan says, calm and quiet and composed, 'That's right. I'm a psycho. And you're all locked in here with me. So I want everyone to be on their very best behaviour, because if you piss me off I'm going to kill every last one of you.'

"And Dunlan turns back around, turns his back on all of them, and closes his eyes again and waits for the doors to open. Six hours he stands there not moving a muscle. By then, everyone else is all over the floor, lying on each other, trying not to crush each other. But they make sure Dunlan's got his space. A little halo of elbow room so no one has to touch him or disturb him in any way. And it's like that until the elevator starts moving again and the doors open on the main floor. The emergency crew's there, and paramedics and maybe a real doctor or two in case people are passed out or worse. But everyone's fine, except for the guy with only one eye, but even he's not complaining. And the owner of the building asks, 'Is everybody okay?'

"That's when Dunlan opens his eyes again and just says, 'Quite.' And he walks off that elevator like the whole trip downstairs took only two minutes. Seriously though, six hours with that many people all jammed together, the medics were expecting to find half of them dead. And except for one of them, they were all in perfect health. They figure Dunlan probably saved lives that day by keeping everybody calm, or at least too scared to panic. Yeah, that's right, Derek Dunlan saving lives. Who'd have thought? Of course the cops wanted to talk to him once they found out what had gone down in the elevator, but by then he was long gone and no one there knew who he was. The last time they ever laid eyes on him, he was heading out the door of the building. And you know what? He was lighting up."

There's a respectful, contemplative silence from the watch dogs. Derek Dunlan stories are the local boogyman stories, and nobody ever wants to be the first to speak afterwards. So I do.

"Last time I heard that one, nobody said anything about Dunlan smoking."

"I told you to stop me if you'd heard it before," says Skiff, sounding hurt.

"Well you know me, I just love listening to your beautiful speaking voice."

I've opened the flood gates, and now the rest of the boys want to know more details, question the facts, reassure themselves that there really is no boogyman.

"Anybody ever seen this Derek Dunlan?" one wants to know.

"Sure, I seen him," is the answer. "Biggest nigger you ever saw. Built like a wall of cinderblocks."

"I heard he was little wop," comes a dissenting voice, "no more than five feet tall, but all muscle."

"Hey, Jimmy! You a wop?" one wants to know of his fellow watch dog.

"Quarter wop. My granny on my mother's side was from the old country."

"Sicilly?"

"Queens."

Their brand of racism is so casual, so familiar, it's impossible to take offense.

"With a name like Derek Dunlan? Bullshit," declares another skeptic who nudges the conversation back on topic. "He's gotta be a mick. Fire-engine red hair and everything."

I have to laugh at these young turks and their old wives' tales. This can go on for hours and I've heard enough of the debate already. Before long, they'll be speculating that Derek Dunlan is a Martian. There's an appointment to keep so I hit the call button for the elevator. My driver steps inside with me when it arrives. He pushes the button for twenty-two, the top floor. I've never been up that high. Accounting is on seventeen, between heroin on sixteen and bath salts on eighteen.

He catches my eye on the button that lights up red.

"Boss wants to see you," he explains.

I've never had the pleasure.

"Really?" I say, flattered. "The penthouse."

He shakes his head.

"One higher."

There's nothing higher.

"The roof?"

"Boss wants to see you pass his window on the way down. Says you've been skimming."

And suddenly the new driver and all the talk of spring cleaning makes sense. I consider bolting, but I know I'll never make it past the dogs, never make it outside, never even make it as far as that stain on the pavement before I've made it a twin.

My hands shake as I reach for the pack of smokes in my pocket.

"Mind if I have a last cigarette?"

"Help yourself."

"Want one?" I offer the driver, trying to hand him one between fingers I hold as steady as I'm able. I'm hoping a bit of courtesy might buy some compassion. If I'm nice, polite, maybe he'll make it quick and let the drop do all the killing.

He doesn't take my offer.

"You said it yourself. I don't smoke."

And as the doors shut us in together, I realized that some of the tall tales are true, some of the ghosts are flesh and blood. And in a day, a week, a year, I'll be another anecdote connected to that underworld boogyman, Derek Dunlan. They'll all remember me and my last words to them over a fire and a story, but nobody will recall the face of the man who rode the elevator back down alone.

It's All on You

WHAT DID YOU DO?

No, don't answer that. It's pretty obvious what you did. And I'm sure you had your reasons. Jealousy, spite, temporary insanity, whatever. It's not important, and I don't really care.

What's important is all this mess and how to deal with it. That's why you called me. That and for moral support, maybe. But we both know people who are better at the touchy-feely stuff. Me, I just get dirty jobs done.

You know what you're asking me, right? You're asking me to be an accessory after-the-fact. That's a twenty-year stretch in a cell right next to yours if we're caught. It's okay, I don't mind you asking. That's what friends are for. But if I'm going to do this thing for you, I need to know you're not going to go soft on me. No offense, but you're kinda soft. You can't be soft now. Not now, not ever. You can't start feeling guilty and call the cops to confess your sins. You can't go and confide in your pals, your buddies, or whoever lands in bed next to you. You'll feel better for a little while, like a weight has been lifted off your shoulders, but it won't last. Twenty years in the can will pile that weight right back on, and you'll spend it all wondering why you ever said anything to anyone after I got you off scot-free.

That's right. I'm going to get you off scot-free, so long as you do what you're told and keep your mouth shut.

You probably weren't thinking straight at the time, but nice work. If you're going to murder someone, doing it near a bathroom is a good idea. Help me drag the body in there and get it in the tub.

You might not want to watch this next part. Hand me the razor. I'm going to open up the neck, ear to ear like so. Now let it drain. Once the blood is out, the body will be much lighter to move, and a lot less likely to splash DNA evidence all over the place.

Don't puke. Do not puke.

Take a breather and start mopping. The bloody soap and water can go down the drain next.

Don't try to put this on me. I know what I said to you. I remember the quote exactly. I told you that if anyone ever talked to me like that, I'd shut them up permanently. That wasn't advice. That was just me saying what I'd do if I were in your shoes. But you're not me. Do you think I'd ever be this sloppy? No, I'd plan my every move carefully. I wouldn't leave a trace. I certainly wouldn't have to call anyone to help clean up my mess.

Nice job with the floor. It's spotless, perfect. You'd never know what happened. So you're done, right? Think again. Look up. See those speckles on the ceiling? You didn't notice those, did you? That's more blood. Spatter from when you caved your pal's skull in. It happens when you keep bashing away. What was it, four, five times? You must have been so angry. Get a step ladder and scrub that down too. I don't care if you ruin the paint. You can slap another coat on once you're sure there's nothing to see and nothing to scrape into an evidence bag.

The body goes with me, along with the murder weapon. It's your own fault for using that pretty sandstone sculpture to do the deed. Expensive was it? Well it's landfill now. Everything gets wrapped up tight in the shower curtain with duct tape so there are no leaks. Wash out the tub thoroughly, pour some bleach down the drain. And get a new shower curtain. If anybody comes by, they'll wonder what happened to it.

That's right. You're staying here. Receiving guests, acting normal, being the neighbourly sort as always. And shrugging your shoulders like an ignorant idiot whenever someone asks after whatshisface. You don't know where he is. And that'll be the truth because I'll never tell you.

What, you think you can't live under the same roof with what you've done? Tough. Suck it up. You move away right after a disappearance like this, people will have questions. They'll come looking. And they won't need a warrant if you're selling the house. All they'll need is a real estate agent, and they're a dime a dozen.

Just remember, we're in this together now. Don't say anything, don't think of saying anything. Because you know what'll have to happen if I suspect you're getting loose with your lips, going soft, getting blabby.

You disappear next.

Underwriter

NICK HELD THE CONCEPT ART at arm's length and had a second, long look. He sat alone on one side of the conference table. His status as odd man out wasn't because he held a seat of importance so much as one of isolation. He was the only one at the table—the only one in the entire third-floor suite—who didn't actually work there. He was freelance.

"So what do you think?"

Nick didn't know quite what he thought yet, so he made a non-committal "Hmm," hoping it would buy him some time.

The head of development tried another approach.

"Any questions?"

Nick figured, correctly, that "Why?" would be too broad, so he narrowed his focus somewhat.

"How old is the kid supposed to be?" he asked, hoping that wouldn't be too probing for the other side of the table.

"He's six."

Nick nodded, suggesting agreement, before he continued.

"Why does he have a moustache?"

There was silence in the room and it lasted too long. Nick knew he'd just plucked a raw nerve. This probably came up in the focus group. It must have. And the entire team had probably just spent the last few weeks convincing themselves it was a fluke and that nobody else would notice or comment.

Ellen, the head of broadcaster relations, shrugged her padded shoulders and explained, perfectly casually, "Because he's Hitler."

Nick flipped through the five pages of concept art again, confirming that the cute tyke featured on each of the boards was indeed sporting a black square of a moustache. The artwork was simple and straightforward, rendered in an aesthetically pleasing and iconographic cartoon style. Easy to animate. The mood was light, whimsical and vibrant. The preliminary drawings had been prepared in a more delicate mix of watercolours. Draft after draft, the art department had received the same note: brighter, brighter, brighter. Marketing wanted the colours to pop. Now that the material was ready to show to test audiences, Nick wasn't sure he could sit through an eleven-minute cartoon at this level of vibrancy without getting a headache.

Once Nick had spent too much time shuffling the boards, Harry, the lead producer, tried to elaborate.

"If he's Hitler, he has to have a Hitler moustache. Otherwise, he's not very…"

Harry searched for a word in vain. Ellen offered one.

"Hitleresque."

"Exactly," Harry agreed. Ellen smiled, pleased to remind him why she made the big dollars.

Nick challenged the concept no further. He didn't make this shit up, he was only brought on to write it once all the ducks were in a row. A small army of producers and storyboarders and in-house directors had been kicking the idea around for the better part of two years. Not to mention their spouses, kids, friends, dry cleaners, dentists and doormen. Only now, with a broadcaster on board and a twenty-six episode order, were they ready to talk to any writers. It was a final step taken with a certain reluctance—seen as a necessary evil in order to have something to shoot. Their eager and able post-production staff looked forward to receiving material to play with. Many of the editors and sound mixers had also offered valuable input during the development process and they were anxious to see the end results of so many lunch-hour and coffee-break conversations.

"Why not Li'l Mussolini? Or baby Pol Pot?"

Admittedly, Nick was being a tad facetious, but the other side of the table had done their homework. Their answer was well oiled, as if they expected to hear this sort of question from a variety of other suits across many other conference tables in any number of office suites.

"It's all about branding. Our market research tells us that Hitler remains one of the most famous names in the entire world. Even all these years later."

Ellen seamlessly picked up the hand-off. "Timing is everything. Right now, we're in a marketing sweet spot. We're at the precise moment in history when the Hitler brand is still instantly recognizable across every conceivable marketplace, but the association with crimes against humanity has diminished with age."

Informally, Harry added, "Those other guys came up while we were spitballing, but they just don't have the same name value."

Ellen nodded in agreement, "We did play around with a Young Idi Amin concept for a while. It had more appeal to certain ethnic minority demographics."

"Blacks," Harry mouthed to Nick from behind a cupped hand.

Ellen continued, "But the market share wasn't enough and it simply couldn't compete with what Li'l Hitler had to offer us."

David, one of the heads of the hydra that ran the production company, consulted his watch and spoke for the first time since greeting Nick with a "hello" and a handshake at the top of the meeting.

"Any other questions?" he asked, not the slightest bit interested in answering anything that might challenge his green-lit project.

Nick carefully considered what his final question should be. He knew his next several months of employment hinged on it.

"When would you like to see my first batch of pitches?"

The corners of David's mouth turned up ever so slightly, and Nick knew he had chosen wisely.

● ● ●

"Was it wrong to take the job?"

"Jesus Christ," cried Sandra, who liked to invoke the Saviour's name, but hardly ever followed his example. "Do you have to ask?"

Nick and Sandra had been married long enough that they no longer needed to ask each other's opinion. Whatever the situation, they already knew it. Sometimes they would ask anyway, just to keep meaningful conversation alive.

"Maybe they'll hate my pitches and I won't be able to sell anything."

Nick knew there was little chance of that. He'd streamlined his pitching technique to the point where he knew he could place a minimum of three episode concepts into any season of any show. They were the exact same three concepts; only the names and places changed. Otherwise, the stories were always identical and he'd sold them half a dozen times each.

"This isn't like those other shows that sell processed cheese spelled with a 'Z' or fruit-flavoured breakfast cereal spelled with a double-O. You know what product you're selling this time, don't you?"

Nick struggled to remember the list of sponsors the advertising liaison had mentioned were a done deal.

"Toaster strudel?"

"Fascism."

"Okay, that too. But not intentionally. Or at least not overtly. It's more of an accidental by-product. Like trans fat."

"Except it kills more people."

"Debatable."

Nick thought Sandra took her principles a little too seriously. Taking a stand on an issue was all well and good until your moral superiority wore out its welcome. It was important to know when to sit down again. If you didn't, you were no better than a vegan, and nobody can kill the mood at a dinner party faster than a vegan. Sandra never let her indignation play out long enough to be a bore at a social event, but she seemed to find this latest project particularly irksome. Nick hoped she didn't go all-out vegan on this one. Maybe, Nick decided, it was just because she was Jewish and didn't think this new show sounded kosher.

"You still meeting Simon for coffee this after-noon?"

Nick was so irritated by the reminder, he forgot to be grateful for the change in subject. He really didn't want to interrupt his day to take a meeting that wasn't going to benefit him in any conceivable way, but he'd made a promise nearly two weeks ago. This Simon person was the brother-in-law of somebody's cousin's friend. For the price of a cappuccino and a bran muffin, Nick would let his brain get picked for half an hour about the ins and outs of the film and television biz. It was a service he provided to aspiring writers on rare occasions, when these meetings were thrust upon him by family and friends he felt he owed favours to.

"Right," Nick grumbled. "That's at one. I'll swing by on the way to the bank, crush his spirit, take out some cash for the weekend, buy milk and eggs. Be back at two, latest."

It was already well past noon. Nick dipped forward to give Sandra a peck on the cheek before leaving through the garage. He made the mistake of looking back long enough to catch her leafing through the pile of Li'l Hitler-related photocopies and documents he'd left on the kitchen table.

"How do you even justify participating in some-thing this morally bankrupt?" Sandra asked in her best tone of rhetorical smugness.

"We have mortgage payments," Nick told her simply, before closing the door behind him.

Sandra took a seat and said no more.

● ● ●

Nick met Simon on the terrace of the local brand-name coffee shop franchise. Everyone there looked like a writer, tapping away on laptops as they paid for their public office space by buying cup upon cup. Simon was easy to spot. He was the only one who didn't have his nose in a computer screen, wasn't scribbling bad poetry into a dog-eared notebook, or thumbing his clever thoughts and observations into a smartphone. Instead, he was people-watching, focused on nothing and no one in particular, letting his attention drift from face to face on the street, listening to clips of conversations and observing bits of behavior in and out of context. Nick felt a pang of concern. As it turns out, this Simon may be a real writer after all.

Simon was young, probably just out of school. Nick took inventory. Wide eyes? Check. Bushy tail? Check. This didn't look good. Idealism was easy to crush, energy less so.

Greetings were exchanged, gratitude humbly offered. Three minutes of niceties was as much small talk as Nick was willing to sit through. As soon as their coffees and sweets were brought to the table, he steered the conversation abruptly to the point. What was it he could do for the young man during their brief time together today?

"I want to be a screenwriter. Like you."

Nick smiled grimly as he poured a pack of unre-
fined sugar onto the fluffy crown of his cappuccino
and watched it sink slowly into the foam.

"Not like me. You want to be a much more
successful screenwriter."

"Well I want to be as successful as I can be."

"You want to write movies."

"Of course. Who doesn't?"

Nick scooped some cappuccino froth into his
mouth and pointed his spoon at Simon.

"Exactly. Everybody wants to write movies. That's
the problem. You know how many movies get
made every year, here and in other English-language
markets?"

"How many?"

"Not many," said Nick. "You know how many
screenwriters and wannabe screenwriters are out there
flogging their spec scripts, or writing for studios on
assignment, or rewriting other writers' drafts?"

"How many?"

"Lots. That's not a precise figure."

Nick thought math was more trouble than it was
worth, but Simon agreed with his calculations.

"Sounds about right."

"It's more than I'd care to count," Nick elaborated.
"More than anyone would care to count. It's like going
to the beach to add up the grains of sand. There's just
no point."

"But I bet there's a point to you telling me this,
right?"

"So when you don't get to write movies, what's the backup plan? Do you quit and get a real job or are you still a screenwriter?"

"I want to write. Anything. I'll write anything."

Nick could see Simon was being earnest, sincere, truthful. The poor dumb bastard.

"Then that's a start. You're already ahead of ninety percent of the other grains of sand. Congratulations."

"Yay, me."

"They're still lying around on the beach getting a tan. Meanwhile, you get to go home with the tourists, lodged in their sandals, stuck in the liner of their bathing suits, or wedged in the crack of their ass. You and a million other grains of sand too stupid to quit."

"So how do I skip ahead of the rest of the ten percent?"

"You hang on for dear life and learn to love the smell of ass."

● ● ●

The meeting ran long. Nick let it. His other errands could wait. By the time he was half-way through his first refill, Nick had decided that Simon was a viable prospect. He wasn't the usual variety of wannabe. He was one of the rare ones who was willing to crawl through that endless desert of broken glass and human excrement to arrive at the ultimate prize the industry had to offer—a bankable career.

Nick decided he was going to fast-track Simon. As a writer, he had no power whatsoever to get him work. But as a writer, he was in the position to offer a hand-me-down. It was the shittiest of the shit jobs, but if Nick had Simon pegged right, he knew he'd jump at it. Just like the professional he wanted to be.

"I'm talking about giving you your first professional contract," explained Nick. "A sub-contract. You won't be working for any studio, production company or broadcaster. You'll be working for me, directly."

Nick didn't fancy himself a mentor. He felt old, but not old enough to mentor someone. Exploit, however, was something he could do. That felt natural enough.

Simon was enthralled by the mere suggestion of employment and immediately went fumbling through his bag, searching for some paperwork that he hoped could seal the deal.

"I have writing samples. Would you like to look at them?"

"No."

Nick let Simon be crestfallen for a few moments before telling him the score.

"Readers read the scripts. Nobody else does. Nobody has the time or the interest. That's why there's a whole job category of people in the industry who do nothing but read the crap writers turn in, and then summarize it for the people who matter."

"How do you handle that? People not reading your work?"

Poor Simon, thought Nick. Still wrestling with career obstacles like pride and ego. Ah well, he was young, new. These things would be ironed out in short order.

"Easy," explained Nick. "I don't actually write the scripts. That's entry-level stuff, even for a screenwriter. How I operate is I keep an eye out for young talent—kids like you—looking to work and make a buck. You do the heavy lifting, I slap my name on it and pay you your cut."

"Wait, I don't get it. If I'm going to do all the writing, what do you bring to the table?"

It was a fair question. Honest, reasonable, utterly naive.

"I get the work. To get the work, you need a track record. I have that track record, you don't. They'll talk to me, they won't let you in the door, because who the fuck are you?"

"But if they saw my work..."

"They won't look at it. If they did, they wouldn't be able to judge it. These aren't literary critics, they're moneymen. What they judge is your track record. That's what they know, that's what they care about. Can you deliver professional work on a tight deadline? That's all that matters. Quality is for artists, and artists make for lousy professionals."

Simon said nothing, didn't try to interrupt. A promising sign. Professional.

"I have a show on right now. Kiddie cartoon. If you want in, you've got the job."

But Simon still looked uncertain. Maybe he had ethics. Maybe they were standing in the way. Nick decided it wouldn't hurt to sell the arrangement a bit more.

"I know the rules of the game, the steps to the dance. I'll pitch some episodes, get them approved, sign the contract. You do the grunt work of actually writing the material—outline, two drafts and a polish, incorporating notes between each step. Maybe one day, down the road, you'll be seasoned enough, connected enough, to branch out on your own. You're looking for a foot in the door, this is it."

Finally, inevitably, Simon asked, "What's the show?"

"It's about the wacky misadventures of a young Hitler, growing up in suburbia and trying to get along with his zany grade-school pals."

Nick thought Simon looked confused. He couldn't imagine why.

"Hitler? As in the Nazi Hitler?"

"You know any other Hitlers?"

Was this a crisis of conscience? Nick couldn't tell. He'd never seen one in the industry before.

"I'm told Nazi-Party imagery will be kept to a minimum. Swastikas didn't score well with test audiences."

His assurances seemed to ring hollow with Simon.

"Still want the job?"

There was only a hint of hesitation before Simon's response, so minimal it couldn't have honestly counted as even a token doubt.

"Yes."

"Good answer."

• • •

Nick was glad Simon had panned out. He had a stable
of young writers he could turn to, but most of them
had moved on, scoring their own gigs, racking up
credits under their own names, earning higher salaries
and harsher headaches. He had been a little worried
that none of them would want the Li'l Hitler sub-
contract, even for some quick and easy scratch. A
promising neophyte like Simon was a timely gift. Nick
needed somebody under his wing—under his thumb.
He was never going to write a word of it himself, not
simply because it was beneath him, but also because it
was beyond him.

Nick was functionally illiterate. He could read the
bare basics to get by, but rarely cared to do so. Picto-
grams pointed him in the right direction in daily life
and he never once walked into the wrong gender's
washroom. Most traffic signs could be identified by
shape and colour. If pressed, he could tell you what
was printed on them, but no one ever pressed. He'd
read a book. Once. It was about a boy named Dick, a
girl named Jane, and a dog called Spot. He remembered the characters did a lot of running around, but
he never finished it to find out where they were all
running to. This dimly remembered tome was very
influential in his work and its themes kept reoccurring

in many of his screenplays. A cute couple, a faithful companion, lots of running around with no rhyme or reason. And a weak ending. It was a formula that kept selling.

Nick's first sure-fire pitch was submitted with new character names and locations substituted to fit the Li'l Hitler story bible that Simon read and briefed him on. A week after the pitch was accepted, he had Simon rewrite it exactly the same, only longer and needlessly verbose. This constituted the outline and it came back with so many notes, it made the modest document three times as long. Simon was given another week to turn that mess into a first draft. After seven solid days of pulling his hair out and finding the common ground between completely contradictory notes, he emailed a draft that was a masterpiece of negotiation and compromise to Nick for inspection.

"It looks great," said Nick, scrolling through the file on his screen as fast as the wheel on his mouse would take him. "Well spaced, correctly formatted. Very professional. I'll assume it's all spell-checked."

Simon, waiting on the other end of the phone line for the verdict, sounded confused. "Didn't you read it?"

"Of course not."

"Then how do you know if it's any good?"

"It doesn't matter. No one who's qualified to make that sort of assessment is ever going to see it. Good, bad or indifferent, it's going to come back with another pile of notes. Notes from the broadcaster, the producers, the director, the story editor… They'll want you to change everything."

"Oh my God. What do we do then?"

"You change everything. And you give them another draft that's well spaced and correctly formatted and looks professional."

"Does that draft have to be good?"

"Nope, because they'll just want us to change it again. Which we will, for what's euphemistically called a polish but is really a whole other draft."

"And that's when we start to make it good," said Simon, a statement rather than a question. He thought he was getting the hang of this. He was wrong.

"No, that's when we get fired. They'll kick us off because no matter what we do to it, it won't be enough. They don't know what they want. They don't know how to ask for what they want. They just think they'll know it when they see it. Which they won't. But eventually they'll run out of time and have to shoot something just to stay on schedule. Probably some Frankenstein-monster hybrid draft that's a cross between our work, the story editor, and whoever else they let have a crack at it. When it airs in a year, you won't recognize a word of it if you watch it—which I recommend you don't."

There was a long, depressed silence on the other end of the line. Nick let it happen. Reality is a bitter pill to swallow. It takes a long time to go down. It takes a lifetime to digest.

"You all right?" he said at last.

"Yeah. Just taking a moment."

"How do you feel?"

"Used."

"You won't always feel that way."

"No?"

"No. Once the cheque clears, you'll feel paid."

"I don't know if I can keep doing this. I feel like a whore. I feeling like I'm squandering my talent. I mean, for fuck's sake, I feel like I'm having a panic attack right now."

Simon was indeed gasping for air.

"Now you're sounding like a pro. Good man. I'm emailing you the story bible for a new show I just got in. Mondo Mephistopheles. Animated, for the six-to-twelve demographic. Have a look, be ready to talk pitches Monday. Early."

Nick hung up before Simon could reconsider his career trajectory.

The Wash

"WE HAVE A SITUATION."

Situation, please. It sounds so dramatic. Mess is what it is. Someone's been sloppy and now they need us to come in, scrub it down and tidy up. An address is all I want. I'll see the details for myself once I know the site is secure and I can do my job uninterrupted.

After every grisly murder, in the wake of every bloody suicide, somebody like me gets a call. I wonder, in the heat of the moment, when some thug is smashing in a guy's head with a baseball bat, or a depressive is sticking a shotgun in his mouth, ready to pull the trigger on both barrels, do they ever stop and think about who's going to clean it all up? Probably not, the selfish pricks.

I pull up outside the house, or should I say House—capital-H. It's not a mansion, but one more wing would get it there. And there's land enough to expand. You'd have to be damn rich to live there, and damn unlucky to die there. Who wants to drop dead when you have a pool, a hot tub and a Jacuzzi to live for? Apparently the owner. Suicide, the call said. I guess money really can't buy happiness. But looking at this place, I would have thought it could make a sizeable down payment.

There are no police taking statements, and no ambulance is parked outside with its flashing lights turning, turning, turning, waking up all the neighbours. Nobody knows what's happened except for me and my mystery caller. If I do my job right, no one ever will.

The door has been left unlocked for me. I knock gently anyway, announcing my arrival to the man who rang. When he lets me in, neither of us says hello. We just nod. We're not on a first-name basis. I don't know his first name, or his last, and he doesn't know mine. We know each other by sight, and that's enough. He works for one of my regular clients, and we've crossed paths at other scenes that needed a quick scrub and a body gone without a trace.

The man shows me to the study without a word. Capital-H Houses all have studies. Small-h houses have home offices. The only difference is how much money gets raked in on those off-hours away from the day job.

I check out the scene and evaluate what has to be done, what supplies and products are going to be necessary, and how much manpower will be needed.

Only then do I call my partner with the list. The suicide was a hanging. They're not messy, but never perfectly clean. I prefer a hanging to a shooting, but there are always released bowels and loosened bladders to deal with. Never assume there's dignity in death, no matter how tidy you try to be offing yourself.

"Standard cleaning products," I report over the phone. "Standard container."

Half a cup of carpet shampoo and a wet vac will take care of the puddle and the smell. The rest will leave with us.

"Twenty minutes," I tell the man who called, and he nods again.

Twenty minutes to erase this problem. I can't erase the life the dead one led, the life that got him to this point. But I can wipe away the death like it never happened. It will be as though he simply vanished from the face of the Earth one day. Foul play might be suspected, but it will be unprovable. Eventually the bureaucracy will get around to declaring him dead just so the estate can be settled, but no one will ever figure out exactly what happened. I don't know why it needs to be that way, but somebody wants it, somebody's paying for it, so it's up to me to make sure that's the way it plays out.

I look at the strangled purple face perched on top of a neck that's been stretched too long. It rings a bell. A big one. It's deafening.

"I know this guy," I say. "Isn't he some sort of lawyer?"

"I guess so," says my anonymous caller.

He's spotted the law degrees on the wall of the study but doesn't seem to care, so I act like I don't either. But he's not just some lawyer. He's *my* lawyer. I saw him in his office downtown only three days earlier. That's a problem. It's a problem because it's close to me, far too close, and I like to keep a professional distance from my work.

Lawyers get depressed too, I suppose. Maybe some of them develop a conscience and the regrets to go with it. Some of them might even go and kill themselves. But I look around and it's not what I see that bothers me, it's what I don't see. Hanging where he is, there was nothing for the lawyer to stand on—no stool to kick away, no chair tipped over. Even the desk is a good ten feet behind him.

"You sure you didn't touch anything before I arrived?"

"No. What's it matter? You're going to make it all disappear anyway, right?"

"Just being thorough," I say. "I need to know if anything has to be wiped down for fingerprints. You never know who might come looking too close once a missing-persons report gets filed."

That seems to satisfy him. He says no more and I keep my mouth shut.

● ● ●

Mack is the name of my partner in crime-disposal who shows up at the scene with my shopping list. We get busy right away. The corpse is cut down and zipped away in a body bag. We wash about three square feet of carpet and vacuum it until it's barely damp. We even drag over a chair so we can brush any remaining rope fibres off the beam where the hangman's rope was tied. By now I'm sure there was a hangman in the room, helping the lawyer commit suicide—making a murder look less malicious.

Once my estimated twenty minutes are up, we've delivered as advertised. Everything's back to normal, if you don't count the absence of one lawyer who should still be occupying the room. Our anonymous caller sees us out and acts as lookout as we load the stuffed body bag into the back of Mack's car.

There are civilian services that do this sort of job. They clean up after crimes and accidents. Somebody has to. Property owners, landlords and heirs don't want to do it themselves, but they sure want to rent out the place again or sell it to turn a buck. So they hire companies that specialize in human-waste disposal. Paramedics take away bodies. Cops take away evidence. But there are always leftovers. Plenty of bodily fluids—and not just blood. Bits of bone, bits of skin, pieces of hair, pieces you don't even want to know what they once were. Professionals wash it all away and make the crime scene vanish. And then the property goes right back to being a place of business, an apartment for rent, a house for sale. New owners, new tenants never know the horrible events that unfolded right under their noses, and they wouldn't want to. Everybody's happy. Except maybe the victims, but they're dead so who gives a shit?

We aren't civilian contractors. We don't do jobs for municipalities or property owners. We're called in to clean up before cops get involved, before paramedics are summoned, before the bodies are even removed. That's because we work for the people who are the cause of the crime scenes—the shootings, the stabbings, and the accidents that weren't accidental.

We make corpses disappear, evidence vanish. We erase history. When we're done with a crime scene, it's like the crime never happened. Stray bullets get dug out of walls, the holes get plastered over. Sometimes we need to repaint the whole room. Soap and water gets rid of the blood. Bleach gets rid of the DNA. Not that that's ever such a huge worry. If we do our job right, no one will even know to look for proof. Still, you don't want to get sloppy. Tiles are the enemy—deceptively easy to clean, but you have to watch those spaces in between. Grout is a bonanza for forensics. It's a sand trap tailor-made to capture and preserve tissue samples, fibres and gunpowder residue. You name it, whatever happened, it's in there and it needs a good hard scrub to get it out.

As for getting rid of the body itself, that's the easiest part, really. Pig farms are good, incinerators are better. Both are always hungry for more and will leave nothing behind once they're done. Ten years ago we splurged and bought a crematorium. It paid for itself inside of six months. Aside from offering us a legitimate cover and a place to launder our money, the oven lets us dispose of just about anything.

There are ashes left over, sure. "Cremains" is what they're called in the business. We ditch them a bit at a time, sprinkle some here and there and mix them in with the ashes of our legit clients. People think they're getting Grandma back in a fancy urn, but she comes with some added-value extras. A handful of Vinnie the Snitch, who got his mouth shut forever by a .44 slug stuffed down this throat; a pinch of Tanya the Whore, who got lippy with a made-man one night and got her head twisted 180 degrees; a dash of Alfonso the bookie, who thought skipping town with the wrong man's winnings was a swell idea until the mob caught up with him and made him tell them where the money was with a ballpeen hammer and—I kid you not—a can opener. Messy ones all. But all swept away now and sitting on your mantel next to a framed photo of Grandma, basking in your love and fond memories. Nice doing business with you.

● ● ●

The caller insists on coming back to the crematorium with Mack and me. He says he's under orders to see the body burnt with his own eyes. I don't question it—this isn't the sort of man you question—but it's way off-script. The clients never want to know the nitty-gritty of my business. Their muscle even less so. It gets me thinking that maybe he wants to see something else back at the crematorium. Maybe he wants to get a look at my collection.

The collection started innocently enough. Spent bullets, murder weapons, gloves that kept fingerprints off evidence, but became evidence themselves when they got left behind at a crime scene. They're all supposed to get burnt in the oven or, if they're too dense for that, dumped in the river. I always mean to do the extra leg work myself, but sometimes there's a backlog and I can't get to it right away when I'm up to my elbows in bodies and blood. One time, about five years back, I got to thinking that maybe I shouldn't get to it at all.

I've always been careful to cover my tracks, but there's still a certain risk of discovery. What would happen to me, I wondered, if the cops figured out my part as an accessory after the fact in so many killings? That's the sort of thing that can put an honest entrepreneur away forever. Several forevers. I realized it might be a good retirement plan to hold on to some of the evidence from the juicier crimes I handled so I would have something to bargain with should the time ever come. Immunity in return for a long list of convictions that would make careers, secure promotions, and earn raises. Any cop or D.A. would gladly cut me loose in exchange for what I had to offer.

It was a terrific plan right up until I let my lawyer in on it. There had been some nosy police detectives sniffing around lately, asking questions. I didn't expect anything to come of it, but just in case, I wanted legal advice, and a set of iron-clad papers ready to cut a deal for my testimony and my cache of incriminating evidence. Now my mouthpiece is dead, and I'm in a car, driving the man who probably did it back to the place where I make problems go away. If he suspects me, I'm probably going to join my lawyer in the oven.

● ● ●

With the oven fired up, I wheel the lawyer's body over in a coffin-sized cardboard box. There's no ceremony, no solemn words, just the rattle of rollers as I push the box into the flames and shut the door. Within the hour, after the flames and the bone grinder have their way with him, he'll be nothing but dust, ready to be evenly distributed among the ashes of the next half-dozen clients.

"Better toss in the ledger, too," says the man who's watching me, and I know I'm sunk.

My collection of evidence, stashed in dozens of safe spots spread all over the city, wasn't worth a thing without context. I kept track of it all—the wheres and whens and specifics of each case—in a hand-written ledger. It was the key to my whole scheme. Without it, I had nothing to bargain with. Evidence without a crime or a context to link it to is useless.

"You mean this, don't you?" I hear Mack say.

I turn around and see him walking towards us with my ledger, normally locked away in a safe I thought I had sole access to. Seeing the book in his hand, I realize how big it's become—a brimming tome of incrimination waiting to happen. It looks heavy.

"Thought I didn't know?" asks Mack when he sees the look on my face. "Who do you think ordered the hit on the lawyer? Who do you think ordered the hit on you?"

I know then that the staged suicide had been staged for an audience of one: me.

"Mack," I begin, "we've worked together for years..."

I cut myself off. That's how I'd exposed myself. Mack did the books, answered the phone, knew my appointments. It's how he must have learned about my meeting with a lawyer, discovered the combination to the safe, found the ledger.

"Wait," says the man who's been sent to murder me, "*you* paid the contract?"

He sounds confused, but Mack is calling the shots now.

"Of course I did," he says. "And if you want the balance, plug my former associate and help me haul the body to the oven."

The contract killer does as he's told and pulls a gun from his pocket. With his eyes on me, lining up his easy shot, Mack takes the opportunity to bring the thick ledger down on his head with as much force as he can put behind it. The gun tumbles to the floor, followed by the man who had just been holding it. I don't question what just happened. Instead, I join Mack on the floor, helping him lift the dead-weight ragdoll before he regains his senses.

There's no time for formalities, not that there are ever many in my line of work. The thug doesn't even get the small dignity provided by a man-sized box. We haul him onto the rollers as-is, dazed and semi-conscious, limbs flailing drunkenly. Mack gets the oven door and I grab our victim by the shoes and give him a shove. There's already a body in the cooker, but there's room enough for two. The door is shut again and bolted before the man knows what's going on. The blow to the head means nothing in the face of that kind of pain. He's fully conscious again in an instant, but it's too late to save himself. I never heard any of the victims I've cleaned up after plead for their lives, or scream their lungs out instead of forming coherent last words. Even so, I expect there's something wholly unique about the type of hollering a man does as he burns to death. A hand, pressed up against the small viewing portal of the oven door, is the last I see of him. His screams stop a few moments later as the flames burn the air right out of his lungs.

"Be more careful who you tell about this," Mack admonishes me, handing back the ledger. "I know it's an insurance policy, but if anyone we work for finds out about it, it's both our asses."

Clever guy, that Mack. I guess that's why I trust him with all the accounting and the phone appointments.

Mack picks up the fallen gun and hands it to me.

"And put this one in the river. Don't keep it as a trophy."

"If you didn't hire this guy, who did?" I ask, hoping he has all the answers.

"Someone who's become a dissatisfied customer," he says.

● ● ●

Yeah, it was a terrific plan right up until word got out about my hobby, and some past client realized my collection of evidence wasn't worth a damn without me to testify about the specifics. Other than that minor detail, I was golden.

I suppose I could run—should run. But I've spent a long time building this business, and I'm not about to start all over again. Instead, I take a good long holiday and hope things will cool down—hope that a suicided lawyer and a disappeared enforcer will be considered message sent and received. I get back to work soon after and it's business as usual.

I don't hear another word about it until I get a routine call to appraise a mob-related shooting. When I walk into a canning factory down by the docks, I'm already calculating how hard it's going to be to wash bodily fluids off all that machinery. Greeted at the door, I'm led inside, away from the street traffic outside.

I don't know the caller's name, but I know his face. More importantly, I know his occupation. He's a hatchet man for the O'Donnells, a syndicate that runs ten blocks in the upper east side. I'm a fan of his work. A bit messy, but thorough. He leaves nothing to chance, always goes for a head shot, two rounds minimum. I have a few of his shell casings in my collection. And that's what worries me.

"Where's the body?" I ask. So far the scene looks immaculate. It doesn't smell of gunpowder. I can't even detect that distinct coppery scent of too much blood spilled.

"You're it," he tells me, and sticks his automatic square in my face. Nobody could miss at that range, and this is a pro.

I have to laugh because it's too amusing.

"What's so goddamn funny?" he wants to know, which makes me laugh even harder.

"Somebody else can clean this one up," I finally manage to say, gasping for air.

I'm laughing so hard, I never even hear the gun fire.

Raw

PEATOR VLADISTOCK IS A TWISTED BASTARD, even among men of his ilk. You can call him Russian Mafia if you really want. He wouldn't even mind. But in this cosmopolitan world we live in, dividing criminal organizations along ethnic or religious lines is becoming increasingly antiquated. There has been a lot of cross-pollination between the gangs, and now you can find flavouring from a variety of backgrounds sprinkled into the mix. The old-timers aren't thrilled by it, but they're all dead, dying, or looking at life sentences that really do mean life. The new guys in charge know better than to turn their nose up at genuine talent just because he didn't grow up on the same street as them back in the day. That's how Peator ended up working as a runner for the Triads in China-town, a bookie for the O'Donnell family in the east end, and an enforcer for the Haitian Reds up north before he went into business for himself.

His success as a criminal entrepreneur was meteoric. After years of slogging in the trenches of middleman illegality—drug running, sex trafficking, loan sharking—he had made all the connections and earned all the fear and respect he needed to become a major player. Within a few months of him branching out on his own he had forced out half a dozen of the weaker hands in the city, claiming their territories for himself.

Why do I know this? I'm not a made man, I don't have "connections." In a city with a vibrant criminal element operating just beneath the veneer of clean streets, glass towers, and a visible police force eager to hand out tickets for trivialities like jaywalking, I like to keep my head down and do my job. But that doesn't mean I don't read the crime reports in the local paper—the lurid police-beat stuff in the back, full of hints and allegations that point fingers in their roundabout way so as not to be legally actionable. Peator Vladistock features prominently at least once a week, but you have to read between the lines because even the most crusading of crime reporters are too scared to cast him in an unflattering light.

My climb up the ladder of success wasn't as storied as Peator's, but I did my share of slogging in the trenches of my own field. Busing plates, waiting tables, short-order cooking, everything you might be expected to do to learn the business. I did eight years as a sous-chef before switching restaurants to finally become a head chef. Ten years later I bought out the owners. I still work the kitchen, cooking my specialties. It's what I love. But now I get to pick everything on the menu, set the prices and reap the profits. It makes for long hours and few days off. I don't have a business partner to pick up the slack, but I also don't have a wife to complain when I come home late every night after locking up and closing the cash.

I was the last one in the place that night when my daily accounting duties were interrupted by a persistent knock on the front door. If any of my staff had been around, I would have sent them to shoo away the latecomer. If the racket hadn't been so loud and stubborn, I would have ignored it. Losing count for the third time in a row, I finally stuffed the handful of twenties back into the cash drawer and shut the register.

There were two men outside. One of them was doing all the knocking, slamming the glass with an open hand, rattling the whole door in its frame. I figured he must be drunk and I wanted to make him stop before he broke one of the panes.

"We're closed," I told them as I approached the entry. I made sure my tone conveyed my irritation.

"Not for us, you're not," said the other man who was overseeing the assault on my door.

When I got closer, I could see this wasn't a pair of drunks looking for a late-night meal to help soak up the alcohol content in their stomachs. Their suits were dark and expensive, their jewelry garish, tacky and also expensive. They couldn't have been more recognizable for what they were if they sported matching uniforms. These were underworld thugs, not to be chased off or denied entry—not to be denied anything if you wanted to keep your teeth in your head.

What they were was obvious. Who they were and which organization they represented wasn't. The neighbourhood my restaurant is located in is run by one of the three major Italian families—the Adinolfis. All I knew was that my protection money was up to date and these guys weren't Adinolfi. They didn't even look Italian. If they were from some other gang trying to muscle in, it would be bad for business. I couldn't afford to pay protection money to two gangs at once while they resolved who was running this block or that street with beatings and a body count.

Reluctantly I turned the latch and unlocked the door to greet the interlopers. To do otherwise would have been rude and conceivably fatal. Maybe they were only here to rob the place. One night's take would be a small price to pay if I could avoid a hospital stay by being cooperative.

"Is the kitchen still open?" asked the one who had been beating on my door.

"No," I told him. "Everything's off. We've been closed for an hour."

"You have a customer coming and he's hungry. He'll want food, maybe a nice bottle of wine. Understand?"

I did. These goons, whoever they worked for, were the vanguard of an entourage. I was already trying to guess which of the major mob bosses had decided on my restaurant for a late-night dinner. I knew this went on—well-respected restaurants opening their doors after hours so some of the power players in the city might have a private meal of the highest quality, away from the prying eyes of the general public. It was a courtesy for crime lords and politicians alike, not that there was much difference between the two.

"I'll fire up the grill, get the oven on," I told the two thugs. There was no telling what might be ordered on or off the menu. I wanted to be ready for any possibility.

"Don't bother," they told me. "You won't be cooking anything tonight."

● ● ●

The car that pulled up outside ten minutes later was black with windows so tinted, they almost matched the body.

I'd been mulling over the roster of who might be arriving the whole time. The names and faces of various bosses flashed through my mind—mug shots on the news, televised appearances at indictments and inquiries. I was trying to remember who was currently serving time, who was facing charges, who was keeping too low a profile to be seen in public, even this late at night. As I narrowed down the list, I felt the terror building up in my gut. Loathe as I was to have any of these high-roller mafia-triad-yakuza types under my roof, most of them could be relied upon to eat, drink, pay and leave in short order. There would be no trouble from them but rather, in all likelihood, a generous tip for my inconvenience. But there was one who was unlike all the others. Trouble was his lifeblood, and murder and mayhem always seemed to follow in his wake.

When Peator Vladistock stepped out of the back of the car, his arrival seemed so inevitable to me, I wasn't the least bit surprised. His patronage was my worst fear realized, and seeing him in person filled me with resigned dread that horrified, but failed to shock.

I watched him pass through my threshold, the door held wide by the toadying retinue travelling with him. He approached me directly, like a nightmare manifest. I felt faint, unfocused, outside myself. The sound of his voice snapped me back into the here and now, much as I would have preferred to be anywhere else at any other time.

"Your restaurant is beautiful. I have heard good things. About the place, about the atmosphere, and about you."

"Thank you," I answered, a hoarse croak.

"The tales of your skill in preparing food have reached my ears and I wish to experience this for myself."

"Whatever you'd like," I said, trying to keep my voice from trembling. "The kitchen is fully stocked, the menu will give you an idea of our specialties. Of course, if you'd prefer something else, I'm sure I could manage just about anything with the ingredients on hand."

"A generous offer. But I have brought my own ingredients. These are for you to prepare and present. You see, I like my meals fresh."

"I assure you, I keep a very fresh pantry."

"No doubt. But my tastes are..."

Peator struggled for a moment to express himself. His English was heavily accented but superb. It wasn't a matter of vocabulary that was holding him up.

"Focused," is the word he finally chose.

I wasn't sure what he meant, but I didn't dare question him. Nevertheless, he could read the uncertainty in my face.

"Have you ever had fresh octopus?" he asked.

I thought about it a moment, trying to remember the freshest I ever had.

"There was a time in a sushi restaurant..."

Peator cut me off, wincing in distaste, "No, not all cut to pieces. Fresh. Alive. Still moving."

I'd heard about that sort of thing but it didn't make much of an impression. I'm a chef. I prepare food. I mix, I stir, I add ingredients, and I baste. Then I bake, boil, roast, fry or fricassee. There's skill and technique and experience that goes into every meal I make. All that dish seemed to require was a fisherman.

"You eat it head first," Peator explained. "And as your teeth tear into its flesh, the tentacles caress your face. It is a very sensual experience. You will never feel closer to another living thing. Not even a woman when you are inside her, yes?"

I didn't know if it was a statement or a question. I nodded in agreement to be safe.

"This is how I eat. How I live. Raw."

Peator snapped his fingers, making me jump. This was a command to one of his men who had come in with him from the car. Peator's soldier was carrying a cardboard box, which he brought directly into the kitchen. His boss gestured for me to follow, and together we walked into my theatre—a pristine arena of ovens and elements, pots and pans, cutlery and food processors. It was one of the very best kitchens in town when I took over the restaurant. After a few costly renovations to bring it up to my personal standards, I was certain there was no finer to be had on the entire coast.

The man with the box set his burden down on a length of stainless steel countertop. He uncrossed the cardboard flaps and opened it so I could have a look inside. Cowering in one corner was a white rabbit. Its pink eyes fixed on me as I peered down at it. It would have bolted if it had the chance, but the box was too deep for it to easily leap free.

"My first course," explained Peator. "A strip from the flank, I would say. Not too much, you understand. The rabbit is small, and is merely meant to awaken my taste buds for something more savory."

I'd never heard of anyone eating raw rabbit before. But, of course, Peator Vladistock did a great many things no normal human would consider.

"Can I at least kill it first?" was my only request.

I didn't relish the idea, but one swift chop with a cleaver would have accomplished the job. I'd done as much to untold hundreds of fish that had come fresh from the docks without their usual fatal nap in a bed of crushed ice.

"Killing taints the meat. You do not wish to spoil my meal, do you?"

"No," I confirmed, knowing this was not a question but a statement. A threat. "Of course not."

Peator nodded knowingly and passed through the swinging door, back into the dining area. He sat at a large table of his choosing and allowed himself to be served by his company. One of his men was already opening a bottle of our finest we kept in a locked wine cellar. No one had asked me for a key, but a bit of property damage was hardly my main concern at the moment.

I had prepared rabbit before, many times, but only ones that had come gutted and skinned from a local butcher who specialized in game meat. Partially skinning a rabbit presented no challenge, nor did removing a choice strip of meat that would hopefully please my patron. But the rabbit was alive and had to remain that way. There would be a struggle, fear and panic—some of it my own. My knife could slip, the course could be ruined, and my life right along with it. I would need help.

The two goons who had first come knocking on my door lingered in the kitchen, no doubt keeping an eye on me, making sure I didn't try to slip away out the fire exit.

"Help me hold it down," I told them. I didn't ask, I didn't request. We were all there at the pleasure of Peator Vladistock, and his happiness was paramount. I was sure they feared upsetting him as much as I did. They didn't complain when I pressed them into service as my kitchen boys.

I hooked my thumbs under the rabbit's front legs and lifted it out of the box. It kicked a few times and struggled to twist free, but I grasped it firmly. Once I had laid it out on my counter, my two assistants placed their beefy hands on the animal and held it in place. It panted in fear, but its struggling abated to a few reflexive twitches once it realized how hopelessly pinned it was.

While the rabbit resigned itself to bondage, I stepped over to my personal knife rack to select one I thought might best strip the furry flesh from a live animal and extract a single serving of meat in as timely a fashion as possible. There were knives and blades specifically engineered for any and all purposes, be it dicing an over-ripe tomato with no loss of juice, or deboning seafood that was mostly bone. Surgeons wish they had tools as sharp and precise as mine. Few could ever hope to be presented with so wide a selection in their own operating theatres. At that moment, I wished my choices were narrower. It was a daunting task deciding which edge would help me skin and fillet a live subject. With the clock ticking and a hungry customer waiting to be served, I went with something small and precise and sharp enough to split a hare.

I positioned myself between my pair of assistants, gripped the short knife resolutely, chose a spot to begin, and committed.

I had never heard a rabbit scream. I didn't even realize they could. Had I thought about it beforehand, I might have expected a high-pitched squeal. But as I cut into its flesh, the sound was more of a deafening squawk. If the rabbit hadn't been right in front of me, I would have thought it was a large bird in distress.

Peator's men hardly flinched. Torturing a poor animal was probably so far down their list of crimes, it didn't even register as any sort of moral transgression. I tried not to think about what I was doing, but instead simply focused on getting it done. The screams were background noise I pretended had nothing to do with my work. I only concentrated on my task, making three quick cuts to allow me to peel back the pelt. I slashed at its underside, easing its parting from the meat and muscle below. Once a decent amount of naked flesh was exposed, I dug in, carving out a portion about three inches long and one across.

"Rabbit sashimi," was a name for the dish that leapt to mind, though I didn't bother to articulate it to my guests.

The screaming finally abated. I thought the rabbit had exhausted itself. It lay limp on the counter, gasping heavily with a broad yawning motion of its buck-toothed jaw. Slowly, my two aides released it and withdrew their hands. Free at last, the rabbit shuddered once, head to toe. Its hind legs twitched twice, still trying to obey the run-away reflex, before it finally expired in front of us.

"I don't hear Mr. Bunny making any noise!" came a call from the dining room. The rabbit's dying screams had been so loud, the whole restaurant had heard. After such a commotion, the silence was deafening.

I exchanged a worried glance with Peator's men. The only course of action was to serve Peator his meal as soon as possible and hope it would suffice—that with the rabbit only moments deceased, he would still consider it raw enough to meet his satisfaction.

I transferred the strip of meat to a cutting board and made a couple of quick trims to make the edges look clean and symmetrical. Then I moved it to a fine china plate for arrangement. A couple of sprigs of parsley added garnish, and a drizzle of my ready-made special sauce left a thin trail around the perimeter of the cut should Peator wish to dab a bite or two. I was careful to make sure none of it touched the meat itself, in case the customer took offence at the idea of any outside flavours influencing the taste of his meal.

I was just ready to whisk the final presentation out to the table when Peator himself burst through the kitchen doors, coming to observe the state of his hors d'oeuvre. I stood there stupidly, plate in hand, as he walked over to the carcass on the counter. He seized the rabbit by the ears and lifted its head up. The rabbit's eyes stared back, glassy and lifeless, and he let the head drop—dead weight on the end of a flaccid neck.

"I thought I made myself clear," Peator said coldly, "My meal is to remain living, even as I dine."

There was little to lose in defending myself now. I confronted Peator, knowing that questioning him about anything was usually a one-way trip to an unmarked grave for most men.

"Is it my fault if it died from shock while I was doing this?" I complained, indignantly. I was hoping the rabbit would shoulder the blame and not get me into any further trouble.

Peator considered this for a moment and announced, "No."

"Fragile creatures," he added, and took the plate from my hand.

For the next few minutes I watched Peator through the kitchen-door portal as he ate his portion of raw rabbit, carefully cutting away small bites with a knife and fork, savouring each piece contemplatively as he chewed slowly and deliberately. As I suspected, he never tried dipping any of it in my sauce.

I was only drawn away from my careful observation by one of my assistant thugs asking a question.

"You finishing that?" he inquired, pointing at the dead rabbit on the counter. There was a childlike expectancy in his face, like a kid who was hoping against hope that Mommy would let him lick the batter off of the egg beaters when she was done mixing ingredients for cake or cookies.

"Help yourself," I said when it finally dawned on me what he was asking.

In short order the rabbit was skinned and beheaded and broiling in my oven. Peator's men rifled through my kitchen on a scavenger hunt that took them through every drawer and cupboard. Lemons, garlic and various herbs were assembled as they improvised a sauce to baste the rabbit with before it was set to cook. At regular intervals, they would check in on their roast and marinade it with juices from the pan using a turkey baster I had never put to use myself. It smelled delicious.

Outside, I saw Peator set his plate aside—clean but for the untouched sauce and garnish. He was chatting with some of his men in an unrecognizable Slavic dialect—probably about business. I wouldn't have wanted to know the details even if I could have understood what was said. He seemed to be in no rush to proceed to the second course. I might have been glad, but he also seemed to be in no rush to leave.

Before long, the two men in my kitchen had also relocated to the dining room. They were huddled around a table of their own, feasting on the rest of the rabbit, and discussing something in an entirely different dialect. They were either talking shop, or telling each other how their families prepared game meat back in their countries of origin. I couldn't say for sure if it was one, the other, or both at once. They were down to the bones by the time the next course arrived.

You could hear it pull up outside.

I'd been left alone in the kitchen long enough to seriously contemplate fleeing out the back way. There was a service alley that let out onto a cross street a block away. From there, I might be able to double back, sneak into my parked car unseen. And then what? Would I ever be able to return to my own restaurant after skipping out on Peator Vladistock's dinner mid-meal? Probably not. Would I even be able to return home after such an uncouth offense? Unlikely. What then? Flee the city, the country? Exactly how offended would he be, and how far would I have to run to avoid his wrath? Was there even such a place so remote, where I could shelter myself from a bad review by Peator Vladistock?

Before I could make a final decision, my avenue of escape was cut off. A delivery van had stopped outside the service entrance. No deliveries were ever made at this hour. The arrival of an unscheduled truck could only mean one thing.

Looking out into the dining area, I saw Peator receiving a text message on his phone. Once he read it, he took a final sip of wine and rose to his feet.

"Part two!" Peator announced, and clapped his hands together.

● ● ●

The truck idled in the alley. It was a standard mid-sized freight vehicle, the sort that gets used for short-distance shipments, moving goods from warehouses to local businesses. The driver hopped out of his cab and hurried to unlock and raise the cargo door. Peator ushered me down the steps at the back of the restaurant, guiding me to the rear of the parked vehicle.

"What is the most exotic meat you have ever prepared?" he asked me. His curiosity sounded genuine. My answer came easily.

"I once took a trip to Beijing to attend a class in exotic ingredients. On the third day each chef was instructed on how best to prepare and present a single bear paw as part of a larger, more elaborate dish."

"Cooked?"

"Baked."

"Pity," Peator frowned. "Ah well, nevermind. This will make you forget all about your bear paw."

Peator proudly presented his second course.

"This I have wanted to try for some time now. It is good for the male vigour, so they say."

The service alley was dimly lit by a few bare bulbs at the back of neighbouring businesses. It took a moment for my eyes to adjust to the deeper darkness inside the truck. Eventually I could make out the shape of hind quarters, a tail, and tree-trunk legs.

"Is that what I think it is?"

Peator only smiled in response.

A woman's plaintive voice echoed in the alley. I looked around the side of the truck and saw a head of long hair hanging out the window of the passenger side of the cab.

"Peator," she whined, "I'm cold."

The door opened and a pair of bare feet dangled outside over the long drop to the pavement. Peator walked over to assist the girl, grabbing a pair of high heeled shoes from under the seat and slipping them onto her feet.

"Of course you are, my dear. There is a chill in the air and you are hardly dressed for a night on the town."

He took her by the hand and helped her down from the truck's high cab. She was young, attractive, and wearing only a simple tan raincoat that must have indeed been chilly that night. I wondered if she was the one who was going to be subjected to Peator's freshly revitalized "male vigour" after he'd had his taste of raw rhinoceros meat.

That was what was waiting for me in the back of the truck—three thousand pounds' worth. It was alive and well, but docile, even dazed. A large tranquillizer dart still stuck in its rump accounted for the animal's mellow mood and willingness to be transported in such cramped, unpleasant conditions. It had been dosed with enough downers to keep it drowsy and cooperative, but not enough to lay it out.

As Peator escorted his young dinner date through the service entrance of my restaurant, he left me with instructions.

"A simple steak, lean. Nothing gluttonous, but a good size."

"For two?" I asked.

"Just one," he grinned. "I always dine alone."

They were both gone a moment later, leaving me with my pair of brutish kitchen boys to contemplate the gigantic slab of meat that had been presented to me. I was already wondering which of my knives could possibly tackle this challenge.

● ● ●

Undoubtedly, the city zoo was currently short one rhinoceros. Precious and rare animals such as this are kept under lock and key at all times, with the layers of security multiplied once the gates are shut and the zoo is closed to the public for the night. Peator would have had little trouble circumventing all the precautions the keepers might have taken to protect their valuable menagerie. If Peator wanted a bite of a rhinoceros, he would have it. Money was the only real obstacle. Money for the manpower, money for the bribes. This would be the most expensive steak I'd ever prepared.

I knew a little about the black market for rhino contraband. Some men in the near and far east still indulged in a pinch of powdered rhinoceros horn to solve impotence problems. Erection pills had stemmed some of the demand in recent years, but there were still those who sought traditional cures for their sexual dysfunction. This was the first I'd ever heard of someone wishing to make an actual meal of such an animal, but as I selected three different viable knives for the task, one of Peator's men swore he had contacts in Macao who would pay top dollar for a taste of rhino if only he could get it to them this fresh.

Once I had my blades in hand—one durable enough to open the outer hide, one sharp enough to quickly remove a steak of tender meat, one fine enough to aesthetically trim what I managed to extract—we three returned to the back of the truck with a flashlight and all the courage we could muster. We took as much time as we dared to contemplate our next move, knowing all too well who was waiting impatiently to be served.

I didn't know which beast I was more afraid of running afoul of—Peator Vladistock or the rhinoceros. If I cut too deeply, caused it pain, startled it out of its doped stupor, the rhino could squash me to jelly against the inside wall of the truck. It would be quick and brutal. Of course, if it was Peator who proved dissatisfied with my skill, the end might be no less brutal, and would probably take a good deal longer. Yes, I decided, Peator was more worthy of my terror. And with that thought weighing on my mind, I stepped into the cargo container of the truck, crouched down next to one of the pedestal hind legs, and sliced into the hide of the gigantic animal with no further hesitation.

I'm sure Peator's organization had unlimited access to every conceivable narcotic bought or sold on the street corners of the seediest parts of the city. Whatever they shot into the rhino must have been powerful stuff. The animal proved to be an excellent patient as I surgically retracted a rectangle of belly hide and extracted a sizable fillet. He only snorted twice, making my heart skip a beat each time, and shifted his weight once, forcing me to pull away from my work and lean back for fear of slipping with my knife or getting crushed.

Once the piece of meat was safely cut from its former owner, I whisked it into the kitchen to be rinsed and readied on a fresh serving plate. The rest of the rhino did not go to waste. Before it was sent on its way, the horn was sawed off and packaged for shipment to an unspecified South-East Asian port where it would be ground into a powder and prescribed by quacks to the extremely wealthy. The animal itself went back to the zoo. Powerful men like Peator have their own private networks to get rid of potentially embarrassing bodies. But rhinos are too big for shallow graves off the highway where rural turns to woods, too big to get mixed in with the cement on some crooked construction site, too big to be ground into meal for the pigs awaiting slaughter at the abattoir. Our rhino was found the next morning, alive and mostly well, tethered to the gate of the zoo. The police and the media would make such a big fuss over the sawed-off horn and the herbal-remedy black market, no one would guess the principal reason for the abduction lay in the hastily-bandaged chunk of flesh missing from the flank. It was ultimately dismissed as an injury from unknown causes, inflicted sometime during the break-in or commute. The crime lab would ignore the fact that a rampaging rhinoceros can't accidentally shave off a tidy little rectangle of flesh, no matter what it might have bumped into. They would ignore it because they couldn't explain it, and nobody paid them for failure to explain. Some of the newspapers mentioned additional minor injuries, but none of them got specific enough to prompt letters to the editor from the conspiracy-minded.

I watched from the kitchen door as Peator indulged in his rhinoceros tartare. I'd been so nervous—so terrified—of cutting into such an enormous, powerful animal, my hands shook and my cuts had not been up to my usual standards. Post-extraction trimming reduced the size of the streak too much and I feared the portion would not satisfy Peator's appetite. The last thing I wanted was to be sent back out to the truck to procure seconds. My solution was to salvage everything, every last morsel, and dice it into a tartare that would serve to tenderize the meat and make the serving appear more substantial. Again my accompanying sauce and garnish were ignored, but at least Peator seemed satisfied with the course.

"What are you bringing me next? A whale?" I grimly asked my helper-watchdogs. Having survived the first two tests, I dreaded what difficulties the third and final dish might bring me. Still, having successfully butchered a live rhinoceros, I felt qualified to tackle their worst.

"I'll give you a hint."

The voice was not one of Peator's men.

"It's smaller than a rhino, but bigger than a rabbit."

I'd become so engrossed watching Peator eat, reading every micro expression, trying to interpret his level of satisfaction, I'd failed to notice the girl who had arrived in the truck. She was standing in one corner of my kitchen, leaning against the wall, holding her thin coat around herself tightly.

The girl offered a hand for me to shake and introduced herself.

"Rebecca," she said. "You can call me 'Third Course.'"

• • •

By the time Peator stepped back into the kitchen, I was in a panic. I frantically rummaged through my mental pantry, asking myself if I had a viable substitute on the premises. What was it they called human flesh, back in the old days, when men lost at sea had to turn to cannibalism to survive? Long pork. It was a possibility. There was pork in the meat locker, entire animals on hooks, just waiting for a skilled butcher to turn them into chops or ham or pig's feet. But they were cold, nearly frozen. There was no time to thaw them, cut a slice, and bring it to just the right temperature to suggest it had been freshly stripped from some unfortunate human lying on my counter.

Without being commanded, the girl, Rebecca, unfastened her raincoat and let it drop to the floor. She was naked underneath except for a simple pair of cotton panties, apparently meant to preserve some small sense of modesty and the integrity of my clean kitchen. Her flesh was smooth and flawless, marred only by needle marks, old and recent, on both her arms, and a tattoo of a butterfly, wings spread wide, on her lower back.

With no discussion, no debate over what it was implied I was to do, Peator ignored me and instead focused on the girl. He circled the finale of his grand feast, looking her up and down, surveying Rebecca as though she were a fresh carcass hanging in a delicatessen window, deciding which cut best fit his mood.

"I think I will have...yes. Give me the butterfly. The ink makes the meat—how do you say—piquant."

Sirloin was the selection, and any chance of passing off a substitute melted away. There was no faking a butterfly tattoo on any other meat in the restaurant. Even if I could fool Peator's taste buds, his eyes would not be deceived.

Peator returned to his table without another word. His pair of scouts who had reserved my restaurant for the night followed him out, leaving me alone with

Rebecca. Even they seemed uncomfortable with this last act, which I'm sure crossed some unspoken line with them that they would never dare verbalize to their boss.

I had dismissed running as an option only an hour earlier. Now it seemed like the only option possible. With the kitchen to ourselves, the back door unguarded, we were free to flee and take our chances bringing this unlikely story to the police. Maybe some of them weren't on Peator's payroll. Maybe some of them would try to do their job and protect us from the criminal madman with the exotic palate.

I picked Rebecca's coat up off the floor and offered it to her.

"Come on," I said. "I'll get you out of here. My car isn't far."

She made no move to retrieve her garment.

"Peator Vladistock must dine," she said. "And you will serve him."

Rebecca walked over to my counter, the same spot where I had unwittingly tortured a rabbit to death a short while ago, and hopped up, sitting on the end. She rolled over onto her stomach, presenting me with the curve of her lower back, and Peator's choice of prime cut.

I couldn't move. Without looking, she sensed my hesitation, could feel me frozen in place several paces behind her.

"You will do this for me. And then I will be free."

I couldn't place the accent, but I could guess at the story. A young girl, born in poverty in some former Soviet-block hellhole. Years spent cobbling together enough collapsed currency to buy a one-way ticket from human traffickers who facilitated that sort of thing with no mention of the strings attached. Were they slick enough to fly her out in an economy seat with a phony passport, or was she stuffed in a cargo container with half a dozen other refugees, rations for an ocean voyage, and a bucket for everyone to shit in? Either way, it wasn't freedom that was waiting for her in the west. It was another agent in the trafficking ring, ready to take a naive girl with no English under his wing, give her food and board and a drug addiction to keep her obedient, and sign her to an unwritten contract to pay off the organization's generosity. And pay she would—probably five times per night on average, with clients who wouldn't be troubled by her overly youthful looks and scant language skills. She would have worked off that debt for years, hardly ever stepping outside of a single room tucked in the back of a massage parlour, never once giving anything remotely resembling a massage. Eventually her English would have gotten good enough to exchange words with the other girls—the other prisoners—in the common-denominator language of the global flesh market. That's when she would have learned the truth from the older ones. The debt could never be paid off because there was no debt. Only fees to collect, night after night, man after man, until she had nothing left that could be sold for quick cash. And what would be left of her then? No wonder she accepted Peator's offer. He'd already taken so many pieces of her, what was one more? At least this final cut would spoil the meat once and for all. The parlour patrons won't pay for girls with scars—especially not with one as horrific as what I was about to inflict on her. Any way you slice it, she was out of the sex trade.

"Do it," she said. "Cut me."

If I try hard enough, I think I can imagine the pain. The cold, piercing sensation as the blade made its first incision. The tug at skin and body fat as it worked its way through to the opposite tip of the butterfly tattoo. The horrible tearing as the window of flesh was pulled away from the muscle and bone it naturally clung to. What I can't imagine is the sort of pain and horror she experienced in the years leading up to this moment that allowed her to bear it so stoically, so bravely. Perhaps she'd already used up all her sorrow and screams long before she ever found herself on my counter, being butchered alive in the name of a late-night snack.

By the time I was mercifully done, her entire body was beaded with sweat. Gulping for air, she collapsed onto the flat steel surface and went limp. Her muscles relaxed, but quivered in shock at random intervals. Rebecca's eyes were red and pooled with bitter tears, but she kept them open, struggling to remain conscious.

"Is it done?" she whispered.

"Yes," I told her, and she blinked once in acknowledgment.

Rebecca was bleeding profusely. Her underwear soaked up the first streams that ran down her back, but quickly became saturated. Blood started to pool on the counter. Before long it was an expanding puddle, reaching for the edges, dripping to the floor, then running off opposite sides in a steady trickle. There was little I could do to stop it, and I didn't dare keep Peator waiting long. I threw a stack of dish towels onto Rebecca's open wound and instructed her to apply pressure while I rinsed the blood off the meat and presented it on a plate.

Rebecca watched my preparations, her face growing pale as she rested her head on the counter. She held the mound of towels at her back, but she was weak and I worried they couldn't hope to stem the flow. Already they had turned crimson, and you could hardly tell they'd ever been white.

"I'll be right back," I assured her. "I'll stop the bleeding and we'll get you to a hospital."

She nodded faintly at me as I pushed through the door and brought Peator his order.

Peator sat with a newly opened bottle of our finest red while he waited for me to deliver the final course. I set the plate down in front of him, making sure the butterfly was right-side up from his perspective. The tattoo was the sole element of decoration. There were no superfluous sauces or sprigs trying to compete for attention this time.

Peator took his time downing a last sip of wine, then cleansing his palate with a mouthful of water which he swished around and spat back into the glass. I made to return to the kitchen at once, but one of Peator's men stopped me with a stare and a slow shake of his head. My continued presence was requested—demanded.

Peator began at the right tip of the butterfly, slicing off a modest triangle of meat and piercing it with his fork. He brought the piece up to his mouth, but delayed tasting it. Instead, he held it not far from the tip of his nose, breathing in its scent. Only once he was satisfied he'd derived all that might be experienced from sight and smell alone did he carefully place it in his mouth and draw it off the fork with his teeth.

Peator chewed slowly and deliberately for much longer than was necessary to pulverize the tiny bite between his molars. His eyes were shut for the entire experience, his mind far away, until he finally swallowed.

Peator's eyes fluttered open again. The protracted moment of his first taste had passed. With his allotted time to delight having run out, he assaulted his meat like a man half-starved. I knew then that the rabbit, the rhino, were mere appetizers. Here was main course before him, and he tore at it with knife and fork vigorously, slicing off mouthful after mouthful, gnashing it with the piston action of his jaw and swallowing hard before each bite was sufficiently masticated.

It took several minutes for the feeding frenzy to pass, and the civil veneer of fine dining to return to Peator's table.

"Come, join me," he said at last.

It was an offer I'd heard from many regular clients who wished to share their pleasure in a well-made meal with the maestro behind it. Sometimes I accepted the invitation, sometimes I brushed it off with an excuse about being needed in the kitchen. This time I was very much needed in the kitchen, but there would be no brushing off this client. Reluctantly I sat down across from Peator.

"How was your meal?" was the standard question that leapt to mind—the only small talk I could muster.

"Exquisite! Each dish better than the last," Peator enthused, wiping the corners of his mouth with a napkin.

"Here, you must try some. You really must," he added, pushing his plate in front of me.

I stared down at the half-eaten strip of human flesh. The right wing of the butterfly tattoo was gone, digesting in Peator Vladistock's stomach even as we spoke. I fought a sudden strong urge to be sick all over my place setting.

"I can't. I couldn't."

"And I said you must," he smiled at me graciously, devoid of warmth or good humour.

I picked up my knife and fork and poised them over the left wing tip of the butterfly. Somehow, after carving a whole steak out of a young woman I had just met, I couldn't bring myself to cut her again—even though the flesh was no longer attached to her.

Peator watched me for a few moments before frustration set in. When he could stand no more of my reluctance, he snatched the edge of the plate and pulled it back to his side of the table. Seizing his own knife and fork again, he cut up my meat like I was a little boy sitting at his father's side, being treated to his very first t-bone. Once the raw flesh had been reduced to nibble-sized chunks, he pushed the plate back in front of me and bade me to try some for myself.

Fork in hand, I carefully selected the smallest piece I could find and skewered it. Following Peator's lead, I shut my eyes and I brought the meat to my mouth, depositing it on my quivering, nervous tongue. I closed my mouth again and balanced the tiny cube of flesh like the act of eating was foreign to me. Eventually, inevitably, a lifetime of conditioning took over and, despite myself, I chewed. Fully aware of what and who I was eating, I had to resist the urge to choke, to spit the morsel back out onto the plate. I didn't dare offend the man I was playing host to. And so I ate, all the while consciously aware of my distaste for what I was being forced to do. But subconsciously... Ah, that's where the primitive, animal-instinct lies. There it is, hidden deep down in the nut-core of our pre-evolved brains. That's where my mouth was getting its command to salivate from—to savour.

My eyes remained shut as I concentrated on the experience. Searching deep, I could detect a slight lavender film of soap from Rebecca's last bath playing across my taste buds. I inhaled deeply and was certain I discovered a hint of her perfume that I had missed in the kitchen. I couldn't hope to identify the make, but rose water was most certainly an ingredient. There was something else I couldn't put a name to. Another subtle sensory input adding to the experience of the meal. It took me a while to pinpoint it, but I got it as soon as I realized it was neither a taste nor a smell I was sensing. It was body heat, ever so slightly above room temperature, but still detectable to a trained palate. Even cut this small, it was still there in the meat, lingering, like the echo of a pulse.

"Well?" Peator questioned me, expectantly.

"Unique," was the one-word review I chose after much consideration. It seemed to satisfy him.

"It is that," he agreed. "My compliments to the chef."

I couldn't look at him. "Thank you," I said, barely a whisper.

"Come," he said, throwing down his napkin, "let us pay our compliments to the meal."

Peator led the way, swinging the kitchen door wide. Rebecca was where I had left her, spread across the counter top. The dish towels I had tried to triage her with were a bloody saturated clump on her back. She was no longer applying pressure. Her arms hung off opposite sides of the counter and the entire area was ringed with a thick pool of deep red that was still expanding slowly across the spotless white floor.

"She's dead," I heard myself say.

Peator nodded in agreement.

"Fragile creatures," he noted.

● ● ●

Peator set a generous roll of bills on his table and weighed one corner down with an empty wine bottle. My tip announced the evening was complete. Without another word, Peator strode to the exit and his entourage instantly gathered to escort him out.

I should have been glad to see him go, but I felt stunned, out of my head, and in my state of shock and dismay I couldn't stop myself from speaking out of turn one final time.

"What am I supposed to do with the body?" I asked like a fool.

Peator paused in the doorway and looked at me, standing alone and lost in my own dining hall.

"That concern is yours, not mine. After all," he said with an unnerving grin, "you're the one who killed her."

Peator passed through the door and out of my life. His men filed out behind him.

I didn't know what would become of me after so strange and horrible a night, but I knew then there was only one word for what Rebecca had become.

Leftovers.

● ● ●

By the lunch-hour opening the next day, the only trace of my late-night diner's visit was a broken lock on my wine cellar door—easily replaced. I'd spent the rest of the night and the whole of the morning cleaning up after my guest and making the rest of Rebecca disappear. I'm no career criminal, well-versed in the destruction of evidence. But I am a master chef with a restaurant at hand, and I know how to deal with food.

The innards were finely diced into tripe, the flesh cut into cubes and left to marinate in bowls filled with the finest oils and herbs and freshly squeezed garlic. The bones I broke up with a cleaver and then boiled to make stock. The softened remains were fed down our industrial-strength disposal unit and ground into a paste fine enough to be washed away through the plumbing.

As for the blood-soaked panties and towels, I incinerated them on a grill, one piece at a time, making sure the vent fans were on full the whole time. Restaurant kitchens get smoky, and the detectors are set to be less sensitive than they are in other businesses, but I wanted to make sure the burning cotton didn't set off the alarm and draw firemen with a lot of hoses and questions. The hair met an identical fate, but made a stronger smell as it burned. I left the fans on to vent the air into the alley behind the restaurant for a full hour and that took care of any lingering odour.

When my staff arrived for the eleven a.m. start, a few noted I'd been in early and cooking up a storm.

There was nothing unusual in that. Nobody questioned a thing.

New specials were printed and added to the menu by the dinner service, with the main ingredients claiming to be anything but what they really were. Piece by piece, bite by bite, my regular customers carried away my crime in their bellies. They left as they always left, happy and well fed, their bodies a little heavier, their wallets a little lighter.

I try not to think about that night, the sounds, the smells, the tastes. My restaurant continues to thrive and has since added a second Michelin star to its rating. For my part, I continue to lord over my prized kitchen and prepare the very best ingredients myself. I rarely indulge in meat anymore, preferring vegetarian dishes for my own meals. And yet, every once in a while, the mood strikes when I'm dining out at the competition or travelling abroad, and I'll order a fillet or a cutlet.

And when I do, I order it raw.

Acknowledgements

The author wishes to thank Kathryn Presner and Michael Brodie for having a first look, and the many publishers and editors who offered homes for these stories in a wide variety of books, magazines, collections and websites.

About the Author

Shane Simmons is an award-winning screenwriter and graphic novelist whose work has appeared in international film festivals, museums and lectures about design and structure. His art has been discussed in multiple books and academic journals about sequential storytelling, and his short stories have been printed in critically praised anthologies of history, crime and horror. He lives in Montreal with his wife and too many cats.

Also by Shane Simmons

Novels

Necropolis
Sex Tape
Filmography

Booklets

Carrion Luggage
The Red Baron: An Ace for the Ages

Graphic Novels

The Long and Unlearned Life of Roland Gethers
The Failed Promise of Bradley Gethers
The Inauspicious Adventures of Filson Gethers

Last Words

Small-press publishers rely on reviews from readers like you to help get the word out about their books. Whether it's a simple star rating or a written critique, every bit of feedback helps convince the impersonal computer algorithms of Amazon, and other literary outlets, that the book you just read has merit and deserves more exposure. Please support independent authors, editors and publishers by taking a few moments to share your thoughts and opinions with other potential readers who may be sitting on the fence about trying an intriguing novel or collection. Your suggestions or comments can make all the difference when it comes to helping them find a new writer they'll like, or matching a struggling author with the readership he or she deserves. Thank you.